MW01128893

This book is a work of fiction. The names, characters, places, and incidents are products of the writer's imagination or have been used fictitiously and are not to be construed as real. Any resemblance to persons, living or dead, actual events, locale or organizations is entirely coincidental.

Knight Ops Series

ALL KNIGHTER

HEAT OF THE KNIGHT

HOT LOUISIANA KNIGHT

AFTER MIDKNIGHT

KNIGHT SHIFT

O' CHRISTMAS KNIGHT

ANGEL OF THE KNIGHT

Louisiana nights can be hot, sticky, and in this case, potentially deadly…

Brainiac Dylan Knight may be a nerd, but that doesn't mean he can't split a hair with open sights at twenty paces. So, when the special ops team needs someone to help bring down a terrorist cell, he's the perfect man for the job. He just never thought the job would lead him to a boutique owner who is as innocent—and enticing—as she is in deep, dark trouble…

Athena Mohamed is no criminal. So, when the government breaks down her door and a stern, insanely sexy special ops guy whisks her away to a safe house, she's confused. The fact that they'd suspect *her* of harboring terrorists is as mind-blowing as her untimely attraction to her new protector. But surely the chemistry between her and Dylan is just a product of adrenaline…right?

They *might* be perfect for each other. They *might* make it to happily ever after. But only if Dylan can clear Athena's name—*and* keep her alive long enough to get there…

Hot Louisiana Knight

by

Em Petrova

Chapter One

"Damn, this feels good." Dylan kicked back on the dock and crossed his ankles. Sunshine warmed his bare shoulders and face, and he closed his eyes for a second, listening to the song of the bayou. Loons, bullfrogs and even the buzz of insects felt like coming home.

"You said it, bro." The second oldest brother Sean stretched out on the dock too, abandoning his fishing rod altogether.

The rest of the special ops force known as Knight Ops reclined in various poses, enjoying the sun or fishing. All of them brothers except Rocko, who might as well be blood by now. They'd adopted him as one of their own.

"For the first time in weeks, I'm not bulked out with gear, and my heart's not pounding because I'm about to take enemy fire," Dylan said with a sigh.

"Incoming." Ben scooped his hand into the water and splashed it over Dylan. He didn't even flinch at the refreshing drops striking his skin. This was the most peace he'd had in many weeks working for the Homeland Security division known as Operation Freedom Flag Southern US, or OFFSUS, and he wasn't going to squander a single second.

The popping sound of a beer can opening made Dylan crack an eye. "Toss me one o' them, would ya?"

Roades reached into the foam cooler and lobbed the beer can toward Dylan, who snagged it from the air. "Just think, Roades, you can *legally* drink at this year's Mardi Gras."

His brother chuckled. "That'll be a change, won't it?"

"Same plan this year?" Dylan took a sip of his cold one. Damn, this day could only get better with some good old Southern barbecue. Maybe that joint down the road was open and they could send the younger peons of the team for a takeout run.

As far as command went, Dylan was smack in the middle of the brothers and the team. But he was willing to abuse his authority—or put one of his little brothers in a headlock—if it meant some good eats.

When no one answered Dylan's question, he glanced around at his two older brothers. "Tell me you guys aren't crapping out on our usual Mardi Gras celebrations this year because you have women in your lives."

Ben and Sean exchanged a look.

"You are."

"Seriously, guys?" Chaz added.

"Well, we can't exactly bring Dahlia or Elise on our usual pub crawl, can we?"

"Why not?" Dylan asked.

Ben raised his brows. "Have you seen Dahlia? Every drunk asshole would be asking to see her breasts so she could earn her beads."

Sean was shaking his head. "No way am I letting Elise do the pub crawl with us. We'll meet y'all for the parade though."

"The parade," Dylan muttered and took another sip. He lowered his beer. "At least I've got two other brothers. Three if you count Rocko, which I am."

Rocko thumped his chest with a fist. "Love ya, man. Truly."

Chuckles followed but Ben and Sean's revelations about breaking their traditional festivities had put a damper on everyone's mood. Dylan set aside his beer and picked up his rod again.

"What if none of us can go to Mardi Gras this year?" Ben asked.

They all stared at him. "What do you know that we don't?" Sean asked.

"I don't know anything. I'm just pointing out that we haven't had time off in a month, and how likely is it that we won't be called in to track some threat across Mississippi?"

"Fuckin' Mississippi," Dylan, Chaz and Roades all said together. It seemed the most twisted missions took place in that state, and none of them were eager to jump when they heard those drawled syllables.

"New Orleans during Mardi Gras is the biggest security threat to the South. Colonel Jackson should just consider putting us on guard duty here." Rocko had a point.

"Jackson won't agree that your pub crawl is protecting the South from domestic threats, Rocko." Ben flashed a grin.

"Look at it this way, you won't have Ben and me, but you'll still have Lexi to deal with." Sean's joke raised groans and growls from all the brothers. Their youngest hellion sister couldn't be trusted on her own downtown, let alone with three brothers as bodyguards at Mardi Gras. After a complication at birth that had denied her of oxygen, she was a little on the naïve side to say the least, though her mouth made up for any shortcomings she dealt with.

"Lexi's definitely not pub crawling with us. And thank God our other sister's far away in basic training." Their sister, Tyler, had run off and joined the Marines without a word, her only goodbye a texted selfie of her shaved head as she attempted to join up as a male.

Dylan missed a nibble on his hook and reacted. He jerked the line clear out of the water, and the hook whizzed past Chaz's ear.

"Watch yourself, bro." Chaz might be the most fun-loving of the brothers, but he had a temper to rival several of theirs put together if pushed.

Dylan looked around at the group on the dock. What had begun as a nice afternoon off was quickly dampened by his woman-whipped or grumpy brothers. Dylan reeled in his line and hooked the

4

fishing hook onto the eye of the rod to keep it from getting snagged on anything in the back of his car. But the rod must have had a weak spot, because as soon as he tightened the line down, the tip snapped off.

The final damn straw.

He jumped up and broke the rod over his knee. Then he stomped to the end of the dock and tossed it in a trash barrel. He reached behind his back where he'd stuffed his T-shirt partially into his pocket and pulled it on. "I'm goin' home," he told the group and strode back toward the path that would lead to the parking area.

With his good mood vanished behind a cloud, he didn't even enjoy the quiet walk to his car. When he rounded a corner and spotted the vehicles in the parking lot, all he could think about was getting out of this dreary place.

His cell buzzed. Only his family members called him, and he wasn't in the frame of mind to talk to them right now, but he looked at the screen anyway.

Ben.

It buzzed four more times. He could go against the rules of the team and ignore the call, and chances were, his brother just wanted to tell him to cool off or something.

But what if Ben wasn't calling as a brother but as his captain?

"Shit." He brought the phone to his ear. "Yeah?"

"Dude, we just got a call from Colonel Jackson."

"Bullshit." He was going to call Ben's bluff.

"No, dead serious. We're on our way out."

He glanced over his shoulder to see the team headed around the bend.

Ending the call, Dylan waited for them to catch up. Knight Ops was his life, and his job was to protect his country against any threats, foreign and domestic. He pushed out a sigh.

He wasn't against going on a mission today, as long as they got back in time for that pub crawl.

For him, it wasn't even about the drinking—he could go without alcohol forever. But it was tradition for him and his brothers to celebrate. Besides, he hadn't exactly met a lot of females during the past month and he was feeling a deep need to get a soft body beneath him. Mardi Gras was the perfect time— have a few drinks, find a pretty girl…

The guys reached him, and Dylan looked to Ben. "Well? Where to?"

"New Orleans."

"What?"

"Jackson got word that there's a threat downtown, a terrorist cell operating out of a clothing boutique."

"At least we're not going to backwoods Mississippi to nail down some asshole trying to blow the state off the map like the past two visits," Dylan said.

6

"They should put it on the visitor's guide," Chaz responded.

They all chuckled.

Ben blew out a low whistle. "Load up, men. Looks like we'll be in the middle of the party. Afterward, I'll buy y'all a round at the bar."

Five cheers went up.

* * * * *

Athena glanced at the ornate marble clock on the shelf. Her appointment was fifteen minutes late, but that wasn't unusual for people with money. She found some of them had no sense of time and came and went when they pleased, and for what Athena made off them during Mardi Gras season, she was more than happy to keep her upscale clothing boutique open later.

She walked to the long bar of dresses, each more extravagant and exciting than the next. All with price tags that could pay her rent for a month.

She resumed straightening each hanger on the rod, putting exactly an inch between each so the whole shop looked neat for tomorrow's opening. She fluffed the ruffles of one Hawaiian red gown with beading decorating the off-the-shoulder detail and considered her late client.

The banker's wife was bold and loved to be seen. And her influential husband loved showing her off. This dress was something Mrs. Landrenau would flaunt during one of the high-class parties taking place all week. The woman relied on Athena's Creations to outfit her for the entire season, and Mr. Landrenau wasn't to be left out of this yearly shopping spree.

I must find a suit to match this gown.

Taking the dress off the hanging bar, she swooped the long, ruffled train over one arm and carried it across the room to the men's section of her boutique. Each garment was either one-of-a-kind designer goods or a creation of her own. And when she'd hand-stitched the beading on this red gown, she'd pictured Mrs. Landrenau wearing it.

Smiling to herself, she flipped through the suits. Pinstripes, lightweight wools. Finally, she came to the more fashionable menswear. Some would call it bawdy, and not at all what a banker would be seen in, but Mr. Landrenau and his wife were the centerpieces of the bank's Mardi Gras float as it rode through Uptown New Orleans.

The white suit with black striped pants and matching jacket would be perfect. She was just hanging the garments in adjoining dressing rooms for the couple to try when she heard the bell on the door tinkle.

Athena drew a deep breath and bundled her thick dark curls over one shoulder, smoothing the soft curlicues that could hardly be tamed in such a humid climate. The frizz around her fingers told her it was a

8

lost cause. Around Mrs. Landrenau, she always felt like such a mess.

Sailing into the front room, she gave her biggest smile. "Hello and welcome!"

The couple turned to her, smiling, looking like they'd just stepped off the glossy pages of a society magazine. Athena greeted them warmly by gripping their hands and leaning in to air-kiss each.

"We're sorry we're late," Mrs. Landrenau began.

"Oh, no matter. I was just choosing another outfit for each of you to try. Tell me, have your plans changed since we spoke last?"

She listened intently to the couple share a list of all their parties and social obligations. Athena had begun working with them months ago, and this appointment was just a wrap-up. But with luck, she'd go home tonight with a little fatter wallet. Between rental space for her boutique and expensive fabrics used for her creations, there were always bills. A little extra never went amiss.

Ten minutes later she was admiring the couple who stood arm-in-arm in front of the three-way mirror. "Mrs. Landraneau, the red suits your complexion so well, and Mr. Landrenau, nobody will be able to take their eyes off you."

His wife turned to him. "You are dashing, Edouard. But I wonder about a top hat…"

Athena jumped to attention. "Oh yes. You're so right. I'll just grab one."

She hurried out to the accessory wall and chose a white hat and a red pocket square for his jacket. When she returned, the couple was deep in conversation. They broke apart and beamed at her.

Athena's arches ached in her high heels and she longed to kick them off and curl her toes into the thick carpet. Heck, she was ready for a nice long soak in her deep tub, but first she had to seal this deal.

"What does the stunning couple think? Is this a yes?" Standing back, she raised her phone to snap a photo of the couple.

"No photos please, though we love your enthusiasm. We see all the photos of people you take and put on social media." Mrs. Landrenau smiled like a model but there was an edge to her voice that made Athena lower her phone. "Yes, we'll take the outfits. I do believe this gown could use a few tucks to fit my curves just right, don't you?"

Athena rushed forward, and another ten minutes were spent pinning the gown. She'd need to make the alterations tonight if she was to get it back to them for tomorrow's events. So much for a long soak in that tub.

By the time she saw the Landrenaus out the door and twisted the locks, fatigue was creeping over her. But she was happy—this was her town and her time of year. Sure, Athena's Creations made money year-round, but this was the Christmas equivalent for her business.

She moved through the shop, tidying up and switching off spotlights on certain creations hanging in alcoves. Then she went into her office and plopped into the chair behind her computer with a drawn-out sigh.

She looked at her computer screen. Too many emails—typical. One from an old friend caught her eye and she skimmed a note about meeting for dinner while she was in town. Um, tonight? She checked a small gold clock on her desk. Not tonight. She dashed off a response and apology to her friend with a promise to have a date later this week after things began to slow in her shop.

Another few minutes were spent checking on purchase orders for special fabrics and sewing notions and then she stood, stretching. Her spine popped in the middle and she yawned wide.

A thumping noise made her jerk, but the sound was silenced immediately. She froze, staring at the door of her office. The rest of her shop was outside of her view, so she popped her head out.

Maybe a shoe had just fallen off a shelf or something.

So why was her heart suddenly hammering and images of a break-in racing through her mind? That was plain silly. This part of the city was safest. She—

A dark figure with another right behind popped into sight. She dodged behind the doorframe, hand plastered to her chest to hold her heart inside. Oh God, she was being burglarized and she had the largest deposit of cash of the entire year right here in this office.

She spun to the desk and snatched up the zippered deposit pouch and stuffed it down her waist, into her pantyhose. Voices sounded, low, in short bursts of commands.

How many were there?

She wasn't taking the time to count. She had one option and it was to dodge into the nearest hiding spot—a small closet crammed with boxes of invoices from former years.

Please don't find me. Just steal all the jewels in the case, smash the glass if you have to. Just do not find me.

Her ears thundered with the beating of her own heart as she stuffed herself into a space next to the boxes. Her hair stood out like a mane, and until now she'd never believed that old story that people's hair stood up in fright. She'd never been so terrified in her life.

Wait—she could call 9-1-1.

She darted a look through the crack in the closet door. Her cell phone was on her desk, where she'd set it down to do her work. Dammit.

Stupid tears stung the backs of her eyes, but she held her eyes wide, refusing to let them fall. She wasn't only afraid—she was pissed. How dare these people break into her boutique and, and... What were they doing? They hardly made a sound and if she hadn't seen them for herself, she would have wondered if she was imagining things.

It was only a matter of time before they ventured down the hall and discovered the office.

She twisted her fingers together and prayed. But her pleas went unanswered. A dark figure entered the office, with another behind him. They wore all black and even had their faces smeared with black paint. They were huge and lumpy, like they carried gear of some sort.

Or maybe they had bombs strapped to themselves.

Don't be ridiculous, Athena, she scolded herself. *What good would blowing up themselves and a clothing boutique do?*

"Take the hard drive while I search the filing cabinet."

She blinked rapidly. Not her hard drive. Did these people realize how impossible it was to keep a business's affairs in order if she lost all her files? She wanted to scream but giving away her position wasn't an option. As it was, she was shocked they couldn't hear her heart pounding or her breathing so hard.

"Wait. Lemme check something."

The closet door broke off the hinges, and she barely got her hands up to keep the wood splinters from coming back on her. A scream ripped from her throat as she stared up into a set of very dark, cruel eyes.

* * * * *

"Jesus." Dylan's muttered blasphemy didn't begin to encompass what he was seeing. A woman, all wild curls and big eyes staring up at him, a scream breaking from her plump lips.

"Fuck, we got one." Dylan reached into the closet.

"Get her outta there," Ben demanded.

Outside the boutique, it had been established that Dylan was the man who could hack the security system the quickest. And that he would go after the electronics and files while the others searched the place. The op was to uncover anything that could lead to tracking down a terrorist. But he never thought Knight Ops would possibly walk into the boutique and find one waiting to be captured.

Or that she'd be staring up at him with big dark eyes.

"Out." His voice was rough, and at first she didn't move. "I said *out*."

She scrambled forward, hands hitting the floor. She pushed to her knees and then a stand, swaying on one high heel because the other seemed to have fallen off inside the closet.

Dylan glanced around. "Sit." He pointed to the office chair, and she limped with as much dignity as a woman on one high heel could to sit down. She

14

looked as frightened as a rabbit—but he had a feeling if she opened her mouth, she'd have a big bite.

Ben leaned over the desk, and the woman's eyes flew wider, if such a thing was possible. She also raised her chin a notch. Damn, the girl had spirit.

"Who are you?" Ben demanded.

"Athena Mohamed, the owner of this boutique."

Dylan swallowed his surprise at her sultry voice. By her exotic looks, he'd expected an accent, but she spoke in a very clear Southern Louisiana drawl, not unlike his *maman* or sisters.

"What were you doing here after hours?" Ben asked.

A crinkle appeared between her brows before she swept her gaze over her desk as if that much was obvious. "Going over the day's finances and purchase orders. Is that a crime now? Who are you, anyway? I'm going to call the police."

Ben gave a short laugh. "Honey, they won't come. This is above their pay scale. Now, tell me right now about what is really going on behind these sparkly gowns and tuxedos?"

"G-going on? I sell them, and right now is my busiest season, as you can guess!"

Damn, there it was again—that sass. Dylan found himself staring at Athena. Hell, that name fit her like a handmade gown.

He snapped himself out of it and stepped up to the desk. "Hand over the keys to anything that has a lock. Including the safe."

Her face turned pink and then red. "If you're going to rob me, then you'd be better off taking the jewelry case. It's worth more than what's inside the safe."

Dylan arched a brow. "We're not here to rob you, lady, but your operations have alerted Homeland Security and now you're under investigation."

Her jaw dropped and all the color drained from her pretty face. "Homeland Security? What for? I haven't done anything wrong! I only sell dresses."

"Sure, honey." Ben's sarcastic muttering had Dylan wondering if his brother was seeing something that Dylan was missing. What if this woman was really just a shop owner caught in the intrigue?

Now wasn't the time to let a pretty face cloud his judgment.

"Hand over the keys." Dylan held out a hand and she fumbled in the desk drawer, coming out with a ring of several keys. He looked at them.

"If you think I'm going to instruct you on which key fits which lock, you're wrong."

The corner of his lips tipped up. "I can figure it out for myself." He ran through several keys and selected one, holding it up. Then he dropped to one knee and unlocked the bottom desk drawer. He'd been on enough missions for OFFSUS that by now he

16

should expect anything to be in that drawer. But what she was actually keeping under lock and key stunned him.

A single pair of shoes glimmering with gems. If they were real, they'd be worth millions.

Or maybe more if they were currency for the terrorist cell.

He'd heard of things like this before. Large sums of money changing hands was easily tracked and authorities tipped off. But a person could find a private buyer for say, a pair of bejeweled shoes, and get what he—or she—wanted out of them.

Dylan hooked his fingers into the dainty straps and pulled out the shoes. He set them on the desktop with a hard clank and the woman flinched.

"What do you think you're going to find here? That's just a pair of heels I've been working on for a client."

Dylan grunted. "These are now evidence. Now tell me the combination for the safe."

She looked about to puke or shoot him with laser beams from her beautiful chocolate brown eyes. When she didn't answer, he braced a hand on the desk and leaned over her.

"The combination." His tone brooked no argument and she spouted the numbers.

His brain locked them in and he circled the desk to the safe while Ben pulled box after box out of the closet. It was so chockful that Dylan wondered how the woman had even squeezed herself around them to hide.

He spun the dial left, right, left and the door flipped open. Inside was a flat bank deposit pouch, empty or nearly empty by the looks of it. And a velvet ring box.

"Don't take that, please." The woman's whisper raised the hair on the back of his neck, and he had no damn clue why that would happen. Hell, he didn't even react after hearing a rifle being cocked behind him, but one whisper had him edgy.

He reached into the safe and withdrew the box.

Ben had stopped removing the cases of files and looked on.

Dylan cracked open the lid, expecting to find something to incriminate this woman as a terrorist on US soil, but what he was looking at were two simple wedding bands made of gold.

He plucked them from the case and held one up, using a pen light to examine it for microphones, microchips or anything else that would give a clue as to why the ring was so precious it had to be protected by a steel safe.

His light flashed over an inscription. *Ou se flè mwen ki fleri nan kè mwen.*

"You are the flowers that bloom in my heart."

Her eyes widened.

"Did you believe a Louisiana boy can't read the Creole, Ms. Mohamed?" The other ring had no inscription.

Ben grunted. "Take the ring and get the hard drive. As for the woman…" His brother turned to her, and she winced, true fear crossing her face. Dylan stared at her closer. She hadn't shown anything but defiance when he spoke to her but she feared Ben? Dylan didn't know whether to be annoyed or flattered.

He returned the rings to the case and pocketed it.

Ben went to the door and signaled to whoever was there to come inside. Chaz and Roades entered, and the woman pressed herself all the way back against her seat, hands tense on the arms as the room crowded with more big strangers.

Dylan moved to stand by the desk as his brothers began carrying out the boxes. When the guys had them all removed, Ben turned to the woman. He stared at her for a long minute. Judging by the way her curls jiggled around her face, she was trembling.

"Should I put her in the vehicle?" Dylan asked.

She jerked.

"Not yet." Ben nodded to the computer, and Dylan set to work. Armed with a tiny electric screwdriver, he had the hard drive out of the device in seconds. Then he took Athena's cell phone too.

"Leave her. She's not connected, from what I see."

Dylan gaped at his brother. His dismissal of the woman had Dylan reeling. Sure, the man was savvy and would never be deceived by a person claiming they were somebody they were not. But Dylan had other feelings on the matter.

"I disagree. She needs further questioning." Dylan wasn't backing down and he wasn't leaving this woman behind. If they were wrong in suspecting her, she'd be released and no harm done. But if they failed to take her and she was a pivotal player in this plot...

Ben shook his head. "She's baggage. We got what we need and it's enough to follow."

Dylan slipped the hard drive into his vest pocket.

Athena reared out of the chair. "That hard drive doesn't go anywhere without me!"

Dylan moved fast, snapping her wrists behind her back and securing them with a zip-tie in a blink. She tugged the bonds, but she lifted her head high, the arch regal and her shoulders revealing that she was a true lady, trained for society.

Who the hell was she really?

He looked her over from head to toe. Something about a thickness around her middle had him dragging her from the chair to her feet. She wobbled on one heel as he patted her down, feeling fine bones and sleek curves.

And an odd shape at her midsection.

He arched a brow, and her eyes shot angry darts at him.

"I need to see what this is," he told her.

She firmed her jaw. "Fine."

He reached into the waist of her skirt, past a tighter band of pantyhose and found vinyl. He extracted a bulging deposit bag and unzipped it to find it stuffed with cash.

"My day's earnings. I'd appreciate it if you don't take the money."

His fingers seemed to sting from the heat coming off her body. For a brief second, his fingers had come in contact with warm, silky flesh.

He shook himself.

"*Cher*, we don't steal money, but this will be kept in a safer place than your pantyhose."

Dylan took her by the shoulder and propelled her around the desk. "Since you're so against being parted from your hard drive, it looks as if you've earned a ride to the interrogation room. Let's go."

Ben followed them out. When Rocko and Chaz looked up from searching the premises, warrior masks firmly in place, they showed no surprise at Athena being led out from the rear of the building. Dylan's face was harder to read as he propelled the obstinate woman around display cases. Amusement, irritation, resolve... all flickered momentarily as the alleged shopkeeper muttered under her breath, her shoulder like granite under his touch.

21

When Dylan reached the back door with Athena, Rocko peeled off from the group. "I'll go with you."

"Give the place one last sweep, boys. Then it's on to Colonel Jackson."

Dylan caught Ben's words as he passed through a back room to the door he'd so easily broken into. He didn't agree with taking the woman directly to Colonel Jackson just yet—he was worried about Ben influencing the colonel and convincing him of Ben's own belief she wasn't involved. She had more to tell them, and Dylan was set on getting it out of her. No way was she innocent in this game, not when the whole boutique smacked of money changing hands.

Apparently it was money that was being used to shut down the Eastern power grid, effectively closing all banks and bringing the whole coast to a screeching halt, allowing laundered money to be siphoned out of the system with no one the wiser. At least, that seemed to be the plan.

Reaching the vehicle, Rocko opened the back door for him and Dylan placed a hand on top of Athena's head to help her duck under the frame. The springy curls winding between his fingers shouldn't give him such a shock of surprise or pleasure but when he removed his hand, he still felt the silky curls on his skin.

"Sit here." He pointed to a seat and she plopped into it hard without the use of her hands and adequate balance. He realized sometime between here and the office, she'd kicked off her lone heel.

He examined her for a moment. Her looks could place her as foreign or Creole or any other New Orleans mashup. Only thing he was certain about was how her beauty hit him like a missile. She hadn't changed her story or wavered at all since he'd found her. Maybe he was wrong that she was involved and was just an innocent caught in the shit storm.

She turned her head to pierce him with her angry gaze. "You're making a mistake. I don't know why you searched my boutique or what is even going on, but you've got the wrong person."

"We'll see." If she wasn't involved in the cell threatening the US, then whoever was using her boutique as a place to pass money into the right hands was going to know soon enough they were found out and Athena would become the target.

"You're sure about this? We can still let her go," Rocko said quietly from behind him.

Athena's gaze drilled into Dylan.

He gave a hard nod. "She goes."

"What am I being accused of? Selling a woman a gown and a matching hat and gloves? Or maybe selling her partner a tuxedo?"

"Don't say another word."

Ben got behind the wheel and the others piled into the SUV. Dylan climbed in next to the woman, far too aware of how small she was compared to him. He must be crazy, but in the past few minutes, he'd gone from suspecting her of being a terrorist to knowing he must protect her from them.

Chapter Two

Who the hell was he to order her around? This was nothing to do with her, just some kind of raid gone wrong.

Athena's mind worked over everything that had happened in the past hour and couldn't shake the shock that left her fingers icy cold.

Or maybe that was the hard plastic that bound her hands together. These men were monsters and the one guarding her like a big dog was the worst of the lot, ordering her around like some kind of animal. Get in, do this, do that. Don't say a word.

The first chance she got, she was calling the police, the mayor and her senator, in that order. She'd outfitted all of them for various events and surely could use her relationship with them to pull strings that would get her freed.

Along with a big apology. Not that a little *I'm sorry* would make up for the fear or indignities she'd experienced. The man had reached down her pantyhose, for God's sake.

And she didn't even have shoes.

The men in the vehicle were silent, their big bodies barely jostling as the leader drove, but she was aware of the man next to her seeming to shift closer and closer every mile they went. She glanced at the small gap between their thighs and drew hers tighter to her body, inner thighs cramping with how tense she was.

He glanced at her and then away. "Port in a storm."

The leader's eyes loomed in the rearview mirror as he stared at the man beside her. The whole SUV seemed to crackle with energy. What did those words mean?

"No fucking way," the leader said.

"Ben, you know what will happen if we go to Jackson. What if we're wrong about this?"

They were speaking in vague terms, but she knew it was about her.

"Port. In. A. Storm." The man beside her couldn't have used a colder tone.

"Goddammit, Dylan."

She blinked. Her guard dog had a name besides Pure Evil or Indifferent Jackass?

"I'm not budging on this. I'm going with my gut."

Silence reigned. Then suddenly the driver named Ben slammed on the brakes and whipped the vehicle around.

"Don't think I won't tell Jackson about this," Ben said.

"Why don't you tell *Pére* too?" Dylan's wisecrack had the other guys snickering.

Athena darted her gaze between them all. Now that she looked more closely, she could see resemblances between most of them. The same brows or eye colors.

Ugh, she shouldn't think of them as human. They'd raided her boutique—they were monsters.

Except now they had names and laughed over jokes.

No, she couldn't allow them to become human in her mind—she was a prisoner, held against her will.

She wiggled her hands behind her back, and Dylan snapped his head to look at her. "Can you feel your fingers?"

"They're cold." Her tone was icier, and he tightened his lips.

"Try wiggling them. I didn't make the bonds too tight and it should be fine until we reach our destination."

Okay, *not* human, still part monster, and he seemed to be the most horrible of them all. How could she be heard? Where were they taking her anyway? What in the world was port in a storm?

After a few minutes, the vehicle stopped. Dylan unbuckled his seatbelt and then hers. He opened the door and guided her out.

"You're sure about this?" Ben asked again.

"Trust me." Dylan's voice was gritty as he took Athena by the shoulder and closed the door. The SUV pulled away.

Darkness seemed to swallow them, but as he propelled her forward, she made out the lines of a building. A house set between fencing with small patches of yard around it.

"Where are we?" she demanded, fear bubbling into her throat. Was he going to hurt her? Leave her here? Panic hit, and she swayed.

He stopped walking and moved to face at her. "Look, we're special ops and the last thing we're going to do is harm you. This is a safe house."

Port in a storm... She was being taken to safety in the midst of the hurricane that had become her life in the past hour.

She stared at him unblinkingly.

"You can trust me." His voice seemed softer, less rigid, less... frightening.

"Am I in danger?"

He didn't answer right away, and she couldn't make out his expression in the darkness. Hell, even in the bright light of midday, she doubted she could discern anything from his stern expression.

Finally, he said, "We need time to figure that out, and handing you over to OFFSUS isn't the right move—I feel it in my gut."

OFFSUS sounded like a very bad organization. And what could he mean about feeling it in his gut? Now her life was dictated by this man's gut feelings? She was about rules and order—her business and life depended on it. The only thing she did on a gut feeling was design work, and even then her logical brain and training would kick in so she could look at the piece she was working on objectively.

"OFFSUS?" she repeated.

He placed a hand on her shoulder and this time it wasn't as hard. She stiffened.

She dug in her stockinged feet. "I'm not going anywhere unless you start giving me answers, starting with your real name."

"Once we get inside, I promise I'll tell you what I can."

She was ready to open her mouth and let her lungs do the talking with some heavy-duty horror movie screams, but that wouldn't get her anything but a sore throat. She went with him to the door, which he unlocked using a keypad.

When they went inside, he snapped on a light, bathing them both in a warm yellow glow.

She twisted away from him and presented her bound hands. "Untie me. Now."

She waited for resistance, but he only said, "Hold still. I don't want to cut you."

A second later, her hands were free. She rubbed her wrists and shook out her cold fingers.

"I'm sorry I had to do that."

She shot him a glare.

He pinched the bridge of his nose as if gathering patience to deal with her. Good—that meant he'd unload her faster and she could return to her normal, busy life and pretend all of this was a nightmare.

"Do you want a drink? The fridge is fully stocked."

She gaped at him. "No, I don't want a drink." Though her throat was parched from all the fear that had controlled her since he'd taken over her life. "I want answers."

"It's me who should be demanding answers, woman."

Why did a thrill go through her when he called her woman? It was disrespectful—it definitely was not hot. But her body seemed to have a mind of its own. Her brain chemicals must be altered for the time being as an aftereffect of all the adrenaline she'd experienced.

He pointed to a few chairs. "Sit."

She eyed the chairs and then his broad back as he disappeared into another room, presumably the kitchen.

Then she darted for the door.

"Don't even think about trying to leave," he called out, stopping her with her hand on the knob. She threw a look at the doorway, but he wasn't visible. How had he known?

He walked back in carrying two bottled waters. "The place is rigged with top-of-the-line electronics and you can't leave unless I want you to. Nobody can get inside either, which is why it's a safe house.

Here." He extended the water and she took it with a scowl.

When she twisted off the cap and brought the water to her lips, she realized how thirsty she was and gulped half of it in one long swallow. He watched her, that heavy stare not straying from her face.

She lowered the bottle. "Now. Tell me why you broke into my boutique, trashed it..." Her throat worked at the thought of seeing all those beautiful, expensive gowns strewn on the floor as she'd been forced out the back door, "and why you've brought me here."

He sipped his water, still eyeing her in that flat way that made her want to gouge out his eyeballs and change his expression.

"OFFSUS is the Homeland Security division in the South. And we were called in because there is terrorist activity at your boutique."

She shook her head. "That's crazy. I sell gowns and tuxedos. In fact, I'm going to lose a lot of money and loyal customers unless you return me right now so I can clean up my shop and be there to open the doors tomorrow."

He shook his head, and she settled a hand on her hip.

"Why not? What have I done? Even your leader— is his name Ben?—said that you could leave me

31

behind, that I'm not involved. Which I'm *not*. So what is your problem?"

That got a raised brow from him. At least he wasn't wearing that indifferent mask anymore.

She pushed harder. "You're opening that door for me." She jabbed a finger toward it. "And I'm leaving. Right now."

"Don't try to order me around, woman. You're under suspicion."

"For what? Selling formulwear?"

"For terrorist activity."

Hell. He was serious, and that made all the blood drain to her stockinged feet. "Terr…" She broke off and felt herself sinking to the floor.

"Oh shit." He grabbed her under the arms and practically carried her to the seating group. She felt the cushion of the sofa under her backside but couldn't register anything but what he'd said. Of course back in her office, she'd understood something bad was going down, but she'd been so angry and upset that she hadn't totally gotten the gist.

Now this man had stated it clearly. They thought she was a terrorist. What was she going to do?

"Do I… at least get a lawyer? My one phone call?" She wet her lips, and his gaze locked on her mouth, tracking the movement.

"Doesn't work that way here."

"How does it work then?" She ran her hands over her curls, trying to flatten them to her head. Her

32

underarms were sweaty, and she'd give anything to be at home right now, pantyhose balled up in her hamper and a cool, silky nightgown on. A bead of perspiration ran down her nape, dampening her hair.

He moved his gaze back to hers. "It works like this—you stay here until we decide if you're a threat or you're under threat."

She was shaking her head. "I have to get back to my shop. Opening festivities are starting right now!"

"You won't be going back anytime soon."

"So what, you're just going to hold me here against my will?" She rocketed to her feet and he leaned back in his chair, looking extremely relaxed and giving the impression that he was far from afraid of her.

She opened her mouth and before she understood what was happening, a scream escaped. The shrill cry echoed off the walls and pierced her own ears. The man leaped up and moved for her, but she jumped back, still screaming.

For his size, he was fast, she'd give him that. He clapped a hand over her mouth and she clamped her teeth together, catching the meaty part of his palm between them.

"Goddammit!" He didn't jerk his hand back, only pressed it harder against her mouth until her teeth started to hurt her own lips. She parted her jaws and he slowly pulled his hand free.

She knew he was bleeding, could feel the warm fluid on her chin. Disgust rose up, but she wasn't going down without a fight. "I want to make a call. Now."

"When you get into a situation like this, woman, you don't get that right. And you'd better not ever bite me again." He made a sudden move that had her cowering.

He went dead still.

"My God, I'd never hurt a woman. I'd never hit you or harm you in any way." He sounded almost injured that she'd think such a thing of him, but he stalked away to the kitchen, leaving her alone for the moment. She raised a hand to her chin and backhanded his blood from it, fighting down the tears stinging her eyes.

* * * * *

Great, now what? Dylan walked over to the kitchen sink and turned on the faucet, letting cold water rush over the bite mark on his palm. Blood oozed from the sharp teeth marks in two perfect crescent moons.

She had good tooth alignment, anyway.

He pushed out a sigh and turned off the water, grabbing a paper towel from the holder. He pressed down on the injury, ticked and impressed at once. She was quick-witted and unafraid of making her own demands. Most people would back down immediately. He'd seen it many times.

Athena was a fighter. But did that make her an integral part of a terrorist cell? He'd grown up with a fighter for a mother and mouthy-as-hell sisters, and he knew strength in women didn't mean they were hiding something.

The bleeding had stopped, and he tossed the paper towel into the trash. Then he scrubbed his face clean of the black grease paint from the mission.

He had a long night ahead of him. He'd need to explain himself and there would be long hours of interrogation to follow from Colonel Jackson. Not to mention taking shit from his brother.

He moved to the fridge. Might as well make some food—he was starving and his charge probably was too.

He pulled out a pack of fresh chicken, some tomatoes and mozzarella cheese. Then he located a pan and drizzled olive oil into it. As he set the chicken cutlets to frying, he chopped the tomatoes into small bits and started some pasta water to boiling.

As he added a generous amount of salt to the water, his phone buzzed. He brought it to his ear.

"Knight."

"It's Ben. What the fuck are you doing, Dylan?"

He leaned against the counter and stared at the meat sizzling in the pan. "Knights always act on our hunches. And I have a hunch."

"A hunch? You have a goddamn hunch? You've taken an innocent boutique woman from her shop and hidden her in a safe house. Jackson's losing his shit over here. I had to listen to him rant for the last thirty minutes."

"You can handle it—you're captain."

"That's not the point," Ben said tightly. "What the fuck are you doing?" he repeated.

Dylan scuffed his knuckles over his jaw, hearing the rasp of five o'clock shadow. Right now, that pub crawl couldn't sound better. He could nearly taste the spice of the bourbon as he tipped it down his throat.

Darting a look at the doorway to ensure Athena wasn't standing there, he lowered his voice. "I can get information out of her."

"You think she's involved then?"

"How can she not be?"

"So you're not keeping her there for her safety?"

"I'm doing that too. It won't be long before these people know her boutique's been raided and she's been taken. They'll know she's at risk of telling us everything she knows, putting them in jeopardy. Which in turn draws a bulls-eye on her back." The complexities were mounting, but Dylan was up for the task.

Ben pushed out a breath into the phone, and Dylan felt all the weight of not only his captain's disapproval but his big brother's.

"I'll answer to Jackson when the time comes, but no Knight has ever been wrong when it comes to our gut instincts, and mine told me to get her out of there and bring her here."

"Fine. I'll give you twenty-four hours and then I'm letting Jackson have you."

"What about the boutique?"

"I left two men on site to wait."

Movement caught Dylan's eye and he looked up to see Athena standing in the doorway, listening. Her wide eyes were luminous, but it didn't look as if she'd been crying. Tough woman.

"Keep me informed," Dylan said and ended the call. Turning back to the range, he flipped the chicken and added pasta to the boiling water. Then he cast Athena a look. "I hope you like chicken caprese."

When she didn't answer, he looked at her. "I'm sorry about earlier. I didn't mean to frighten you."

She swallowed hard, her slender throat working. "How's your hand?"

"Fine."

Ever since opening that closet and setting eyes on her, something odd kept rising inside him, leaving him feeling off-kilter. "Why don't you sit down and I'll answer some of your questions while I finish the food."

She stared at him. Her face a perfect oval, her skin flawless. Dark eyes were framed by thick lashes and a small beauty mark rode just above the corner of her upper lip. And that hair... He clenched his hands into fists, still feeling the silky curls under his fingers.

A high counter sported two stools and she hesitantly crossed the kitchen to sit on one. His attention was drawn to her shoe-less feet, and remorse hit him. He'd have to get her some shoes as well as clothing if he was going to keep her here.

She folded her hands before her, back erect as she waited for him to speak.

"My name's Dylan Knight. I'm a member of the Knight Ops team, and we operate here in the South."

"Why were you told I'm a terrorist? What on earth would I be doing?"

"I can't disclose all the information to you for obvious reasons."

She rolled her eyes, which coming from one of his sisters, might have made him laugh.

"So you just assume I'm mixed up in some terroristic something or other and arrest me."

"You're not under arrest." He stopped short of adding, "Yet."

The chicken was finished and he removed it from the heat, sprinkling in the tomatoes and wishing he had some fresh basil. Finally, he topped it with the mozzarella and placed a lid over it to melt while he waited for the pasta to cook.

"I'm under watch, is that it?" she asked.

He gave a nod, arms folded across his chest. They sized each other up, and damn if his body wasn't liking what he saw. From the steely backbone he saw in Athena to the feminine ruffle of her blouse against her warm tan skin, he admired her. Actually, he was having a hard time looking away from her, and that was dangerous, given he hadn't had a woman in far too long.

Dammit, he should be in the city right now, buying a drink for the next woman he'd be taking to his bed. Instead, he was sitting here tormenting himself with a beautiful woman who was out of bounds for so many reasons.

She looked down at her fingers twisting together. "What do I do about my business?"

"It's closed. Seized."

Her gaze flew to his. "Seized? Does that mean I can never open it again even when I clear my name? I have no idea what you imagine is going on there!"

He lifted a shoulder in a shrug, feeling for her. "I can't answer those questions, but for now, you're closed for business."

* * * * *

Athena's stomach couldn't feel more knotted than it did at hearing that she wasn't going to finish out the Mardi Gras season or serve those customers who were counting on her.

And when she thought about the pricey shoes that had been confiscated from her desk drawer, not to mention the wedding rings that had belonged to her late parents, her throat closed up and she couldn't get food past it if she tried.

Though what Dylan set before her smelled delicious, her stomach felt hollow.

He set a plate before himself on the counter across from her but didn't sit. "You should eat before it gets cold."

She stared at the meal, which looked like something out of a food magazine. Did the man have to be talented *and* good-looking? He was her captor, keeping her here against her will and ruining her livelihood. Athena's Creations depended on those high-paying customers to stay in business and if she didn't open, she'd get a bad reputation.

She compressed her lips and took deep breaths to calm the panic rising inside her. The heavenly scents of tomatoes and mozzarella only had her stomach waking up. She hadn't eaten in many hours, and this sure beat the frozen dinner she'd have at home in front of the TV.

Her stomach got the better of her, and she picked up her fork. The gooey cheese clung to the tines and she brought it to her lips. A groan nearly escaped as hunger took over and she dug in, forking bite after bite into her mouth before she realized she must look like a wild animal.

She stopped and glanced up at Dylan, who was looking at her with a mix of concern and enjoyment on his face.

Her fork slipped from her hand and clattered to the plate.

"I take it you like what I fixed."

She didn't respond.

"I'm starved, so I hope you don't mind if I eat while I question you." He wrapped his fingers around the fork, and veins snaked up his hand and forearm. If she wanted, she could follow them all the way to his heart, but that would mean asking him to take off his shirt and she definitely should not want that...

He took a bite and chewed, studying her without pause.

"What's your ethnicity?"

Annoyance hit. "What is this—an ancestry website questionnaire?"

He cocked a brow.

"If you're asking if I'm American, yes, I am. I was born here, as was my father. My grandfather was an immigrant, but so was everybody's."

He nodded. "That's true. An immigrant from where?"

"Are you probing me to see if I have ties to some country with known terrorist groups? Because I'm not."

"Ah."

Ah? What the hell did that mean? She folded her arms, food forgotten.

He continued to eat, his motions surprisingly elegant, and she was shaken by her reaction to him. If she'd met him at any other place than breaking down her closet door, she might have let that spark of interest take hold. But he was a monster, pure and simple.

A monster who could cook.

And who looked like a god with his chiseled jaw darkened with beard growth and eyes that seemed to look right into her.

Something akin to liquid heat slid into her belly, riding too low to be indigestion.

"Tell me about your clientele."

She straightened. "What do you want to know? That they come into my store packing automatic weapons and flinging money around that they're given from their terrorist group to purchase expensive clothing they will wear when they bomb the next major city?"

His lips quirked at one corner. She stared at the spot, and her brain registered amusement in that expression. Was he laughing at her?

"I don't know what you want me to tell you. I told you I don't know why you raided my boutique or why I'm even here. I'm innocent and I'd like to go home."

He polished off his chicken and set aside his half-eaten plate of pasta. Figured the man wouldn't even eat carbs. He probably chewed up nails for breakfast and followed it with gasoline right before raiding daycares and terrorizing all the little children.

She glared at him.

He withdrew his cell from his pocket and set it on the counter between them. She looked at the photo there. "Why don't you start by telling me about these?"

The shoes she'd put thirty hours into creating, each gem hand-set with tweezers in the perfect positions to catch the light. Her client was a socialite with high-end taste and a budget to match. She'd married a man forty years her senior who showered her with gifts and gave her everything her heart desired, which happened to be the shoes Knight Ops had confiscated.

Along with her hard drive and those precious heirloom wedding bands, dammit.

She folded her arms and stared at him.

"What would you like to know? That the shoes are worth half a million dollars? Or that the woman who ordered them from me will be in tomorrow to pay the second installment for them and pick them up? Or that I won't be there to get the money *or* give her the shoes?" She tapped her nails on the countertop.

"Why don't you tell me about the gems. Particularly the blue ones."

Her brows drew together. "What are you talking about?"

"The blue gems — did you order them from someplace or were they given to you by the client?"

43

"What the hell are you talking about? I ordered them." Her mind worked over the details and her heart dropped so fast that it hurt. The client had given her a photo of the exact blue gems she wanted on the shoes and had even provided her with a website to purchase them through. Half of the deposit had gone directly to purchasing those gems, some of the most expensive Athena had ever dealt with.

Rattled, she gripped the countertop.

Dylan was staring at her. "Say what's on your mind, Athena."

"I don't know anything about those gems other than they're expensive and beautiful and they make the whole design." She was exhausted, confused and pissed off beyond measure.

She hopped off the stool, angrier that she wasn't wearing shoes, and shoved the stool in until it banged off the counter. "Am I allowed to go to bed? Or am I supposed to sleep locked up in some dungeon?"

"I'll show you to your room."

She threw up a hand to stop him from coming near her. She couldn't trust herself not to bite him again. "I'll find it."

She strode from the room with as much dignity as she could in stockinged feet that couldn't even make a sound with her stomps. She followed a short hall that led to two bedrooms and she took the largest. Let Dylan feel cramped and claustrophobic.

First thing she did was go to the windows and try to open them, but they seemed to be sealed shut.

She released a growl of frustration and stormed across the room to lock the door. Then she threw herself on the bed. She needed to find some shred of control in this huge mess, but the longer she laid there, the angrier she became.

Dylan had thrown a big question into her path, and she didn't know how to answer it.

What if the client who requisitioned those special shoes had set her up? And what could those blue gems possibly be if not extravagant details for a spoiled trophy wife?

She only lay there for a few minutes before getting up again. She walked into the kitchen to find him cleaning up the mess. Dammit, she didn't want to see him performing these domestic tasks like a... a human being.

She folded her arms around her middle and waited to wake up from her nightmare. But after several long seconds, she was still just standing in the middle of a strange house with no shoes on.

Dylan turned to watch her. She met his gaze head-on, anger spiking inside her all over again.

"Look," he rubbed his hand over his short hair. "I'm sorry at the way you've been treated. This isn't what we do, ripping women out of their closets and throwing them into vehicles. Now this." He stretched his hand to indicate their surroundings.

45

She didn't respond to his words. He and his team had terrorized her, and she wasn't going to forget that very quickly.

"Will you sit so we can talk?"

"You mean interrogate me some more."

His expression changed from the stern asshole he was to something she couldn't wrap her head around. He looked... contrite.

He took a seat, leaving her standing. "Let me explain what's happening the best I can without telling you classified information." He waved at a chair, and she reluctantly took it. Once she lowered onto the wooden seat, her muscles that had been screaming with tension seemed to turn to jelly.

"We don't operate on our own, so when you think of us barging into your boutique and tearing it apart—harshly, I might add—it is because of our orders."

She gave a light nod though she didn't totally get any of it. The who, what, whys of the entire ordeal were beyond her understanding.

"I can't explain more. Just know that we are not the monsters you think we are. We were just acting on orders, doing our jobs. Whether or not you're involved—"

"I'm not." She set her jaw.

His gaze traveled over her face as if searching for the answers in her features. She stared right back

46

until he gave a nod. "Okay, maybe you can tell me more about those shoes."

Here we go again.

"I told you they're for a client. She requisitioned them as an original creation."

"But such a pricey item would be kept in the safe, surely."

"They were inside a locked drawer, if you'll recall. And in my world, that is enough. I don't have break-ins or clients who would shoplift when they have the cash in hand."

"Fair enough." He sat back against the chair and all of a sudden, she saw him as a man and not the beast she had up until that point. Conversing with him in a more civilized manner was showing her things she wasn't certain she was ready for. She was still furious about what had been done to her and her shop. And she wasn't going to forgive so easily just because he suddenly looked human.

In black cargo pants and a black T-shirt that fitted to his muscles like a second skin, he was still intimidating. Actually, if she met him on the street, she would only look twice because of his size and the way he carried himself, with the presence of a god.

He sat there for a few minutes in silence. Finally, he looked up at her. "I'm sorry for the trouble, miss."

She'd been taught to accept apologies with grace, and she automatically responded with a nod and a murmured, "All right."

47

"No, it isn't. The more I think on the situation, the more I realize the colonel acted on intel and you were just caught in the crossfire."

"When are you going to believe me in saying I am not involved in what you believe I am. I'm a business owner and a designer. I have a simple life that I fill with my love for my work." She paused, realizing this was getting her nowhere, repeating — over and over — the same mantra of innocence. Or ignorance, as the case may be. Resigned, she said, "Is there a bathroom for me to wash up besides this one off the kitchen?"

He jerked to his feet. "Of course. I'm sorry. I should have showed you where it's at earlier. This way."

He walked through the living room to a short hallway leading to bedrooms and a bathroom. He knew his way around the space, leading her to believe he'd been here with others before. She didn't want to think about that, about what other women were being accused of terrible things or that there was so much danger in the city she loved.

She washed her hands and splashed water on her face. Looking in the mirror, she saw the creases of strain around her eyes and thought of how she must look to Dylan. Not that she cared, but the way he studied her so closely made her wonder if he still had suspicions.

It wouldn't be the first time her looks had earned her questioning. In airports, she was often stopped. Wrong or right, it was something she lived with. In time, she believed the United States would stop fearing all the people who looked like they hailed from that part of the world that had been responsible for the attacks of 9-11.

She leaned against the counter and fought against the constant worries hurling themselves at her brain. How to get out of this situation? She only wanted to go home and get on with her quiet, yet happy life. And what about her shop? It was a disaster, and she'd lose so much money at her most important time of year.

Realizing all she had was her wits and determination, she walked out of the bathroom and into the living room where Dylan sat. He looked up at her entrance, and something passed over his face.

Something almost vulnerable.

She didn't understand such an expression coming from him, and she raised her chin a notch as she walked up to him. "I'd like to leave now."

"I can't let you do that."

"Am I under arrest?" she asked for the second time.

"No, you aren't. But you're deep in this sh—" He broke off on the curse, as if she was too sensitive to harsh words that she only wanted to use herself. "Pardon, miss. My *maman* taught me better. You're deep in the middle of this situation, and I promise to return you home as soon as it's possible."

In other words, she was wasting her breath.

He stood and gave her a penetrating look. "I give you my word, Athena."

Her belly gave a small tremble at his use of her name.

"I guess I have no say and no choice in any of this."

His eyes were almost sad as he looked into her eyes. "I'm doing what is best for you. I can only say that I will give you your life back when it's time."

The *when it's time* hung in the air, unsaid.

The man might be trying to lure her in with kind looks and softer-spoken words, but that didn't mean she was buying it.

Chapter Three

Dylan's thumbs moved over the burner phone. Replying to Ben about what was going on here at the safe house took all of two sentences.

My charge is calm. She hasn't changed her story.

He threw a look at the closed bedroom door. When he'd asked about those gems, the expression of blank shock on her face wasn't something people easily faked unless they'd been trained extensively to cover their reactions. Dylan had seen it before, and he didn't like that he couldn't get a read on Athena.

Ben must be busy because he didn't respond. So Dylan pocketed the phone and quietly walked to the bedroom door. His hearing was excellent, but he didn't detect a sound from inside. He stood there a long minute, wondering if he should knock and ask if she needed anything.

Hell, he might ask just to hear the sharp edge of her tongue one more time. Her spunk amused him.

Deciding he should leave her be, he turned toward the living room again just as a crack of thunder shook the house. A muffled noise from within made him jerk his hand up, prepared to break in the door if necessary.

The choked sound cut off and silence reigned again, though the rumbling growl of thunder went on and on. Another streak of lightning lit the place, and in that old trick his *pére* had taught him for figuring out if the storm was getting closer or moving away, Dylan began counting.

One-one hundred, two-one hundred. Three —

Another loud boom hit, and he listened closely at the door, but no sound reached his ears.

The storm went on and on, raging like it only could on the Gulf. Dylan moved away from Athena's door a few more times, only to be brought back by another thunderbolt so intense that he was sure she might need something.

He wasn't going to contemplate why he felt the urge to stand guard this way like some protector.

His shirt clung to his spine, the sticky air not even cut by the air conditioning, and he pictured her on the bed, pantyhose balled up on the floor and her legs bare. Maybe even sleeping in her bra and panties.

His mouth dried out.

He'd been around a lot of beautiful women, but he'd been trained to be aware of every single thing in every single moment, and right now he admitted Athena stirred his blood in a way he hadn't felt in too long. Maybe it was only because he was a horny motherfucker, but he didn't think she was just any other woman.

Dylan had reminded Ben that a Knight always followed his gut, and right now it was screaming that

Athena was the most desirable woman he'd ever set eyes on.

He sank to the floor outside her door, leaning his back to it. With one leg outstretched and the other hitched up, he slung his arm around his knee and let the noise of the storm roll over him.

As a kid he'd always loved storms. Then he'd experienced battle and quickly those placid tones of thunder had transformed to something to be feared in his mind. He'd heard of fellow Marines being thrown into PTSD episodes during storms, but luckily he was okay.

He rested his head against the door and let his mind wander back to those summer nights in his childhood bed when he'd listen to the thunder, Chaz and Roades not far off in the bunkbed. Sometimes Roades, being youngest, would get up and pad down to their parents' room to crawl between the sheets with them and gain comfort, but Dylan would lie there and listen to the fury of nature.

When another flash of lightning lit the hallway, he thought of how Athena would look in the bluish light, those dark curls highlighted to the color of a raven's feathers.

His cock twitched with the need to sink into her, to claim her as the world raged around them.

Port in a storm. Hell, his thoughts of keeping her safe were going off the rails.

Thunder vibrated the house again, and a thump behind the door had him leaning away from the door. It flew open and Athena tripped over him. She went down hard—or would have if he hadn't caught her.

The air whooshed from her and then she struggled against him, only managing to tangle her legs more with his. As lightning streaked down again, Dylan made out her features. Parted lips, wide eyes, the adorable slope of her nose... and enough hair to wig two women and a child.

Her eyes grew huge as she realized he was holding her cradled against his chest and his thigh rode high against the V of her legs.

"Get off me!" Palms on his chest, she pushed away. She rolled onto her stomach and then got to all fours.

He gazed at the roundness of her ass. "Jesus," he muttered, launching to his feet before he could grasp her hips and yank that beautiful behind back into his groin.

His cock throbbed. Damn, this woman was giving him a run for his money. He reached down for her hand. When he pulled her to a stand, she folded her arms tight over her chest.

"What are you doing out here?"

"Protecting you."

"Guarding more like."

God, that sassy mouth was the equivalent of flint to steel. It had been a very long time since he'd had a spirited woman. Most saw how he looked and fell into bed with him with very few words exchanged, and Athena was refreshing as hell.

The storm seemed to hit a fever pitch, and he wasn't coping very well with the burn in his groin either. He ran his fingers through his hair, thinking up something to say, but she turned and headed to the kitchen.

She was fully clothed though her legs were bare, he knew from the scorching heat he'd felt through his cargo pants. He fixated on her backside until she bent over to retrieve a bottled water from the refrigerator.

He tore his gaze away. "Sit down."

"Why?" She looked about to bolt back to her room and lock herself in again.

Probably not a bad idea if she knew the dirty thoughts circulating in his mind.

He placed a hand on her shoulder. She flinched, and he drew away.

"When my brothers couldn't sleep during a storm, my *maman* would make us hot cocoa and a special snack."

She eyed him, that adorable crinkle between her dark brows begging for his lips. He wanted to feel the worry smooth away and then look into her eyes before claiming her mouth.

"Trust me." He waved to the stool again, and she reluctantly took it.

Sometime while they had been sleeping, the power went out, but he had a flashlight with a strong beam. He switched it on and set it in the center of the countertop so the halo of light struck the ceiling and lit the space better than a candle could.

He went about fixing the cocoa and a snack. Bread, peanut butter, grape jelly. He placed the sandwich on the plate and began cutting off the crusts. He didn't glance up but felt Athena's gaze following him. And fuck no, he wasn't going to admit the way it tightened his insides.

When he pushed the plate across the counter to her, she stared at it.

"PB&J with the crusts cut off," he said.

"I know what it is. I've never had the crusts cut off before."

He lifted a shoulder and let it fall. "It's how my brothers and I liked it." He mixed up some hot cocoa for each of them and placed two steaming mugs on the counter.

"I always liked PB&J as a kid." She lifted the triangle to her lips.

"I know."

She froze before she bit off the corner. "You know?"

He studied her face. If he told her that he could find out more in a file than she'd ever want to disclose to any other human, she'd hop off that stool, run to her room and lock the door faster than he could draw breath.

But he couldn't lie to her either.

"I'm known as a brainiac among my team. I can find things out."

She dropped her sandwich to her plate and glared. "How?"

"I'm good at uncovering information."

"So you read people's grocery lists from their trash."

The laugh took him by surprise. It escaped his lips before he could bite it back, but damn, it felt good. He shook his head. "No, I don't do those things. But there's information on everybody in the world if you know where to look."

She shoved the plate back at him as if by eating it, he'd have some advantage over her. She leaned her elbows on the counter. "Do you know my father's name?"

"Mohamed Mohamed."

She smacked her palms off the counter, frustration taking over her pretty features. "My car make?"

"You don't own a car. You take public transportation."

Angry heat glimmered in her eyes. If the light had been better, he might not have been able to keep going in the face of that anger, but he was feeling a bit reckless too.

"How about my date to the senior prom?"

He fished out the name from the file locked in his brain. "Sam Marsh."

A half-scream, half-moan rose from her. "Oh my God, what don't you know? Don't answer that." She snatched up her sandwich and took a two bites, rapidly chewing and then swallowing. She took up her mug and sipped.

He found some cookies and offered her one.

She snatched it up and threw it at him. It bounced off his chest and hit the floor, crumbling on the tile.

He fixed her in his stare.

She scrambled off her stool and backed up.

He circled the counter, stalking her all the way across the room until her back struck the wall. Dylan was a little ticked at not understanding who this woman really was in all of this—and wholeheartedly aroused.

Bracing his palms on the wall on each side of her head, he leaned in. She tipped her face up, boldly meeting his gaze. "Athena, I don't know what role you play in this game, but I am not treating you badly, am I?"

"Cocoa and a sandwich don't make up for you taking me out of my shop and forcing me into this safe house." Her voice held an edge that only set his blood racing faster.

He dipped his gaze to her lips. "The cookie doesn't make up for it?"

58

Her breaths came faster. "You know what I thought about the cookie."

Grunting, he resisted the need to swoop in and claim those plump lips, to swallow all the sassy words she used to combat him in the only way she knew how.

"*Cher,* I am not the enemy — know that."

"What are you then? I don't want to be here, and I've done nothing wrong."

He studied her expression, confused by the way her eyes dilated. Fuck, he wanted to kiss her until she was gasping. Then thrust into her until she was screaming his name.

"Athena, I run off gut instincts, and all my alarms are saying I need to keep you here."

"I'm in danger?" Her words came out too soft, too breathless.

Yeah, in danger of him ripping off all her clothes.

* * * * *

As Dylan leaned over her, the storm was drowned out by the thunder of Athena's heart. His spicy male scent ignited body parts she'd forgotten she owned, sending a smoldering heat down between her legs.

God, she could still feel that hard thigh of his wedged there when she'd fallen over him in the hallway.

"I won't let anything happen to you," he said.

She stared at his angular jaw, so shadowed with beard growth that it could no longer be considered scruff. In the few hours between finding her in that closet and now, he'd sprouted a full-on beard.

Her eyes threatened to slip shut, and she bit off the feminine sigh that his good looks roused in her. She must be out of her freakin' mind. Maybe this was what Stockholm syndrome felt like—didn't they all claim they were protectors and not captors?

Except she *was* being accused of terrorist activity.

Her head told her to duck out from under his arm and break for her room. So why was she standing so still, rooted beneath his dark gaze?

"I can't let anything happen to you." His warm breath washed over her lips. A string pulled tight between her nipples and her pussy, a bolt of need with more energy that any lightning the storm could bring.

Oh God, he was hovering so close, his hard lips a scant inch away. If she went on tiptoe, she'd be able to see if his mouth was really as hard as it looked.

And if that beard was rough.

"Dylan..."

"Athena. Hell, I want to kiss you."

He did? Her mind stuttered to a stop, and she closed her eyes, waiting for it to come.

But it never did. Five heartbeats later, she opened her eyes.

His stare zapped her with electricity. She barely registered his movement before his mouth slanted over hers, landing with all the hard need she'd read in his eyes.

A soft moan left her, and she angled her head. He took immediately advantage, parting her lips with his tongue and sweeping it inside her mouth. Another moan escaped, more primal this time.

Raised as a lady, she should be horrified at how she sounded right now, but she'd forgotten how to care about anything but Dylan's taste and the feel of his mouth moving over hers.

She raised a hand and grasped his shirt, balling the fabric in it. He planted a hand on her lower back and swayed her away from the wall, bowing her hips to meet his even as he plunged his tongue deep.

Tremors started in her core and spread out through her entire body until she was tingling with want. She must be insane, reacting to all the fear she'd felt the past six hours. This definitely wasn't her.

Okay, she wasn't so prim that she couldn't kiss a handsome—okay, *hot*—man back. But he was a stranger, a brute who'd put her in a situation she did not want, even if it was his job.

He moved his fingers in small circles up her spine, leaving heated tension with each warm pass of his fingertips. Another crash of thunder shook the house, and suddenly Dylan jerked away.

Breathing hard, he glared at her as if she'd been the one to initiate the kiss.

She ducked under his arm and took a step back.

"Fuck. I'm sorry." His arms hung at his sides. Damn, his appearance punched a hole through her, all carved muscles and the strength of two men. And he roused the desire of two men as well.

Confusion claimed her mind, taking all the words with it. She held his stare for another heartbeat before turning away and going back to her room. She closed the door quietly and leaned against it, thinking how good she'd felt in his strong arms while the storm raged around her.

* * * * *

Fucking hell. Why had he kissed her?

His body was asking a totally different question, though—why hadn't he picked her up and taken her to bed?

He blew out air through his nostrils and stared at where she'd last been standing.

He wasn't one to take advantage of people—ever. And it didn't set well with him that his desires had overcome his control. Ben would hand his ass to him and Colonel Jackson would have him court martialed for his actions.

Only he wasn't about to tell them. Would Athena tell?

When he thought of her soft lips under his and her body pressed so tightly against him, he only felt her need, not fear. She'd kissed him back with as much enthusiasm, but he still had no excuse for what he'd done.

The impulse to return to her door and sit outside was strong, but he couldn't guarantee he'd be able to keep from knocking softly and asking for entry.

The storm was beginning to die down, the thunder moving off in the distance. Rain fell more gently. As he stood in the kitchen, contemplating his actions, the power restored and he moved to shut off his flashlight.

Athena's plate and mug were still on the counter, and he took them to the sink. The cookie crushed under his boot, and he shook off the crumbs with a smile.

Damn, the little wildcat had gotten enough guts to throw a cookie at a man who outweighed her by a good hundred pounds and had been trained to be a killing machine.

He moved to the living room and stretched out on the sofa, a step up from the floor in front of her door. He listened hard for any noise coming from her bedroom but only heard the rain pattering the windows and roof.

His mind was too exhausted to work over the puzzle that was Athena — whether or not she was working with the people they were trying to bring down was something he'd have to leave until tomorrow.

The pillow beneath his head was lumpy and he tossed onto his side. Then returned to his back again. Finally, he tossed the pillow to the floor and tried using his arm, but no way was he going to fall asleep. There was another bed, but he couldn't trust himself with only a wall between him and Athena. At least this way, he had to take enough steps to reach her that he'd come to his senses before walking into her room while simultaneously unbuckling his belt.

Maybe not.

His cock throbbed behind his fly at the scenario he'd conjured, and now all he could think about was Athena's skin glistening with perspiration as she rode him nice and slow...

Fuck. He sat up and then gained his feet, standing for a moment, undecided. When his cock gave another hard twitch, he sprang forward. There was a bathroom off the kitchen and he'd at least have some privacy if he had trouble swallowing his moans.

He navigated in the dark, his vision supreme, and barely closed the door before he whipped open his jeans and reached into his briefs for his hard cock. Wrapping his fingers around the base, he squeezed. Eyes closing at the sensation of pulsating need.

Part of him knew he was acting like a horny animal, but he was a man in his prime and he'd gone too long between lovers.

No, he was not totally losing it over this woman who was his charge.

In his mind's eye, he undressed her. Starting at the dainty buttons at her throat and moving all the way down between her breasts, dipping his fingers between the fabric as he went.

He stroked his cock from base to tip, a groan at his lips. Fuck, he needed to stroke hard and fast to get this out of his system, but the images flooding his mind were too damn good to ignore.

Dropping his lips to hers, sinking his tongue deep into her sweet mouth and tasting her rising desire. Then peeling off her top and skirt to reveal the fancy lingerie he knew she must wear, judging by what she carried in her shop.

Perky breasts.

A moan passed his lips as he rolled his swollen cock head through his fist.

Laying her down and parting her round thighs.

Jesus, he was going to blow any second.

A thumping noise made him fall still, though it took more willpower to stop his fist. He breathed hard in the small enclosed space, his orgasm right *there.*

Another bump and then more that could only be footsteps.

And Athena didn't have any shoes.

"Goddammit." He shoved his steely cock back in his underwear and zipped his pants. When he stepped out of the bathroom, the Knight Ops team was standing in the kitchen. Roades bent over before the fridge, pulling out containers.

Chaz grinned. "Forgot to flush, dude."

"I didn't get to finish. What the fuck are you assholes doing here?" Blood raced through his system, and he felt all his veins standing out, snaking down his arms.

Roades shut the refrigerator, cutting off the light in the room.

Ben stepped up. "There wasn't time to mess with a call or text. We need you and the woman out of here. Now."

Dylan's brain caught up to his brother's words. "Why?"

"If she doesn't open her shop tomorrow, it presents more of a problem to all parties." Ben eyed Dylan as if he knew every dirty thought in Dylan's mind since he'd set eyes on his charge.

"Meaning if she doesn't open, the people who are involved will know something's up and she becomes more of a target."

"A target with a beautiful face and great hair." Chaz bit off a precooked sausage and chewed.

"Hey, don't underestimate a lot of hair. Great for pulling or pinning to the bed." Roades held up an unpeeled carrot and bit it off.

Dylan clenched his fist, prepared to knock his mouthy brothers on their asses.

Ben closed his eyes momentarily. Finally, he opened his eyes and stared at Dylan. "Get the girl and meet us outside. You've got five minutes."

The room emptied as Knight Ops filed back out the door, each carrying some food Roades had swiped and leaving Dylan standing there wondering what the hell he was doing.

He shouldn't be in the middle of this at all. If he hadn't insisted on bringing Athena to the safe house in the first place, he wouldn't need to worry about getting her back safely to open her shop because she'd already be prepared to do that.

Her shop.

If she was opening those doors tomorrow, they had a lot of work to do tonight to right what they'd destroyed inside when tossing the place.

There weren't any options.

He walked through the house and rapped on Athena's door. She answered immediately, and his cock hardened more at the sleepy rasp of her voice. Five minutes wasn't enough time to do anything with her, even steal a kiss, because once he started, he'd never stop.

"Athena, we need to move you again."

The door flew open and she stood there, eyes wild. "Where? Is there a threat?"

God, now he wanted to pull her into his arms and press her head to his chest and whisper that it was going to be okay.

Him? Whisper? He was a fucking Marine with the mind of an intelligence officer. He could hack a man's entire life and then turn around and shoot him between the eyes from half a mile away.

Whatever this woman was doing to him needed to end—now.

"We need you back at your boutique. You have to open it in the morning."

"My—Are you kidding? I can't open so soon after you guys tore it apart!"

His gaze centered on her hair, and Roades' words filtered into his brain again. Good for pulling, pinning to the bed.

Fuck.

"We need to go. Did you leave anything behind?" She was still fully dressed minus the pantyhose.

She gave him one of her trademark looks that he was beginning to recognize as her gearing up to open her mouth and give him the sass.

"Do I look like I have anything to leave behind? You ripped me out of a closet and I don't even have shoes."

He did feel bad about that, but his experience with his sisters was that if you gave them thirty seconds to complain, it wouldn't stop for a very long time.

Grabbing her by the elbow, he drew her out of the room and led her down the hall. At the front door, he

68

looked at her bare feet. "Do you need me to carry you to the vehicle?"

She blinked rapidly and then said, "I'm fine."

As he closed the door behind them, he mentally scoped the house. He'd walked in with exactly one woman and was going back out with her. He did still have the burner phone in his pocket, though.

The black Knight Ops SUV sat waiting for them in the shadows. When they approached, the side door opened and he urged Athena inside. Then he dropped the phone to the ground and stomped it hard, smashing it to pieces. He kicked them into the gutter and climbed in.

"We saved you some cheese." Roades reached over the back seat and extended a block of cheese still in the wrapping.

Athena glanced back like she couldn't believe her eyes, but Dylan barked out a laugh. Leave it to his brothers. As kids, their *maman* said they could eat even if the world was coming to an end.

He took the cheese and held it out to her.

She shook her head and faced forward again, arms wrapped tight around her torso.

Hell, he really was hungry as hell. Did she realize how delicious her breasts looked thrust upward like that?

Chapter Four

As they drove through the familiar streets of New Orleans, Athena was surrounded by big intimidating males. The city was still alive with activity—Mardi Gras was a nonstop celebration.

Next to her, Dylan shifted for the third time. Good—she hoped he was uncomfortable.

A wrapper crinkled and the man behind them tossed the plastic at the back of Dylan's head. It fell over his shoulder to hit his lap, and she saw the wrapper from the cheese he'd handed back after Athena refused it.

She shook her head again. Not that she knew what to expect from a special ops team, but they seemed weirder than normal.

Dylan smashed the paper in his fist and stuffed it into the pocket on the seat in front of him. "What's the plan?"

Ben... and was it Sean?... cast him looks over their shoulders.

"You can speak in front of her. She needs to know what's happening, doesn't she?"

She gripped the edge of the seat until her fingers grew cold, waiting to hear their responses.

"We've got all the equipment you need in the back. Jackson's orders. You set up on the premises and she opens tomorrow as usual."

"How can I open Athena's Creations when it's trashed? It will take me days to clean up." She thought of all those gowns lying trampled on the floor. So many things had to be destroyed. Plus she had alterations to do for Mrs. Landrenau, and that woman did not like being kept waiting.

Tears threatened the backs of Athena's eyes, but she refused to let her emotions kick in. She had work to do, if what they were saying was true.

Minutes later, they pulled into the alley behind her building. Just hours ago, they'd burst in her back door.

When Dylan got out and extended a hand to her, she glared at his fingers—they were far too callused for her liking anyway—and refused his help.

He stepped aside to allow her to exit the vehicle while Ben opened her back door again.

"Wait a minute—is that my key?" She bit off the words that felt like acid on her tongue. Her father used to tell her that she let her temper get the best of her too often, and Athena had worked hard to master that. Now no matter how many times she counted to ten—backward and then forward—she was still seething.

71

When she walked into her store and switched on the lights, all the suppressed fury rose up. She threw her head back with a strangled scream.

Silk and satin gowns were strewn across the floor, some with boot prints on them. Accessories were dumped all over the glass counters and shoes lay in disarray. She mourned a sparkly rhinestone buckle that lay smashed near her bare feet.

She whirled to face the men and picked out Dylan among them. "There's no way I can clean this up to open by morning!"

"You don't have an option." He stared at her, his expression as stern as ever. She balled her fists. Why had she ever let him kiss her?

Then the other guys started carrying in boxes and Dylan directed them to her office. She waved at their broad backs cloaked in black.

"What are they doing?" she demanded of Dylan.

"I'm setting up surveillance. Did you think you were opening alone? Everything that happens in this shop, every word that is spoken, every look given, I will know about." With that, he walked away, following his team to the office.

Her office.

In a fit, she kicked a dress out of her way and ran after them. What she saw made her pull up short. High-tech devices being unpacked from boxes, along with tools.

"I need holes in every wall," Dylan instructed.

Her jaw dropped. After a full twenty seconds, she snapped it shut and found the words lying like volcanic rocks on her tongue. "Holes for what?"

He didn't look up from the camera in his hand. "How do you think I'm watching your store without cameras?"

"Are you serious? You can't just punch holes all over the place and install cameras. If you're trying to be covert, you're not doing a very good job."

The guy known as Chaz sniggered, and Dylan shot him a dark look.

Athena stood there waiting for answers, but nobody seemed in a hurry to provide them.

Finally, realizing she wasn't going to get what she wanted, she spun on her bare feet and stomped into her shop. She switched on a few lights in the front section of the store and set about picking up gowns and putting them back on hangers. The longer she worked, the angrier she became.

What exactly had those men been searching for? Did they think she had a collection of bombs hidden among the boning of the bodices?

Just as she hung up the final gown on the rack and stood back to note how wrinkled everything was, Dylan and Chaz emerged from the office. Dylan pointed at a spot high on one wall and Chaz took a hammer to the drywall.

She screamed.

They turned to stare at her, and she lowered her hand from her mouth to spew all the words pent up inside. She strode up to Dylan and stabbed a finger at his chest. "Give me that hammer because I'm going to punch a hole in you! What am I supposed to do to hide that? My customers don't want to believe they're being watched! These aren't teens in the hood!"

He fished into his pocket and came out with a nail. He handed it to Chaz, who nailed it in above the hole. Then Dylan strutted over to the clothing rack and took down a gown. He carried it back and handed it to Chaz, who hung it on the nail, covering the hole.

Athena set her hands on her hips. "Seriously? How does that even help you? Can your cameras see through fabric?"

He twisted his mouth in a way that made her want to punch him. But she also remembered how good those lips had felt moving over hers, how much more she'd wanted after pulling away.

"Don't worry about our methods. You'd better get to work—there aren't many hours left in the night."

She bit off another scream and the following rant that bubbled to her lips. Spinning, she lit into the shoe wall next, cursing under her breath as she had to match each pair and inspect them for damage before placing them neatly onto the shelves.

Meanwhile, the men crawled all over her store. Each time she heard that hammer breaking through

74

her drywall, she ground her molars harder. She was helpless, at their mercy, and there was nobody she could call for help in this matter right now.

Although, she had plenty to say as soon as the opportunity arose.

"Put it right there."

She turned at Dylan's deep voice, trying not to think about how hard her nipples pinched at the mere sound of it.

Then she saw what he was instructing Chaz to do.

Athena dropped everything and walked over. "What are you doing?"

"This device has to sit on your counter near the register."

"Oh sure, that military surveillance device won't look out of place in this boutique. Are you going to stand by the door with your arms folded and glare at all my customers too? Because a bad ass dude who screams military won't seem weird at all." She shoved her curls behind her ear but as usual, the thick mass wouldn't stay and fell forward again.

Dylan's eyes roamed from her hair to her face and back again. At his fierce expression, she stopped mid-tirade. Her stupid heart picked up the rhythm.

Then he dropped his gaze to her mouth, and she… she…

What had she been thinking about?

Oh yes, she wanted to knee him in the balls for looking at her like he wanted to eat her up slowly.

She curled her toes into the floorboards and tried to harness her raging hormones.

"You think I'm bad ass?"

She blinked. Was he seriously looking for an ego stroke right now?

"Ugh." She turned away and pushed the device he'd placed on the counter back at him. "Take this away."

"No need. I thought of another way." He withdrew a small screwdriver from his pocket and as she looked on, popped the cover off the device. He deconstructed the unit right in front of her eyes, spreading the small parts out across the marble counter. Then he picked up several and began fitting them back together in a new way like a kid with Lego toys.

What the hell? This man wasn't just delicious biceps threatening to pop the seams of his T-shirt or shoulders that could rival most NFL players'. When he'd begun setting up the surveillance system, she hadn't considered he was a tech genius.

He caught her staring and gave her a crooked smile. And damn if that didn't slide straight between her thighs and nearly draw a groan from her.

"The guys call me a nerd, but I don't mind. I can build just about anything from a little bit of nothing."

From several feet away, his brother Chaz called out, "And hack anything. Even the Pentagon."

She nearly choked on the air she was sucking in. "The Pentagon?"

"That was years ago," Dylan muttered, focused on the intricate parts he was forming into a device no bigger than a fat beetle. He straightened and held out the device on his broad palm. "Is that too detectable now?"

"Um…" God, she felt all shivery now. A handsome guy with muscles for days was great. But a handsome guy with muscles *and* brains?

He was giving her that crooked grin again, the corner of his hard mouth cutting up into his cheek and creating a smile line she wanted to trace with her fingertips — right before she kissed him.

Okay, she was sleep-deprived and distraught. Losing it now was not an option.

"It's fine." Her voice was too faint for her liking and with her phenomenal luck, Dylan would realize how he was affecting her. After all, he must get it all the time.

He looked at her more closely, and his brows etched together with concern. "You look tired, Athena. I'm sorry you didn't get more rest before we dragged you back here."

She stiffened. Irritation washed over her. No woman liked to be told she looked tired. They wanted to hear they were beautiful and fresh-faced goddesses. She snapped her mind shut on any softening toward him.

"Thanks for letting me know."

She resumed her work and fought to ignore the man standing far too close for comfort. He might be five steps away, but she could almost feel the heat coming off his body not to mention that kiss they'd shared in the heat of the storm...

After conquering the shoes and then part of the jewelry—some necklaces were hopelessly tangled and would take her days to put to rights—she leaned against the counter and stared at her shop.

Things were looking better, though later she had to do something about that dress hanging on the nail high on the wall supposedly concealing Dylan's camera. With luck, she might be able to open in... three hours.

She glanced to the windows at the storefront and saw the first glimmers of shapes as the night began to brighten from black to shades of gray.

Someone nudged her arm.

She looked up to find Dylan standing there balancing a tray of coffees on one palm and gripping a big bag. From the heavenly scents of yeast, she could only guess it was donuts from the bakery down the block.

"Oh my God. I never get these." She grabbed the bag and peeked inside. Glaze ran down the sides of puffy donuts. She reached in and pulled one out. "The bakery's always closed by the time I get here."

78

"Gotta come in the middle of the night. I almost didn't get any either—Mardi Gras has everybody roaming the streets late."

She really must be dead on her feet, because a smile broke over her face as she bit into the donut. The dough melted in her mouth and sweet glaze hit her tongue. She moaned.

When she saw Dylan staring at her in that dark way that made her inner thighs tremble, she lowered the donut.

His gaze locked on her lips. "You've got... some glaze." He sounded as if he'd taken a bullet and was trying to mask the pain in his voice.

She swiped her tongue over her lips, and he growled. In one step, he was up against her, pulling her into his firm body.

"God, I want to kiss you again. Tell me I shouldn't kiss you again."

She couldn't think of how to form those words. "I..."

"Hell." He swooped in and crushed his mouth over hers. Licking over her lips and then thrusting his tongue inside. She barely had a chance to wrap her mind around it before he was withdrawing.

He stepped back, chest heaving. Somehow, the man was still balancing the coffees and he set them on the counter to run his fingers through his military-short hair.

"I'm sorry," he said.

What did she say to that?

"Thanks for the breakfast."

"No problem. I didn't know how you took your coffee, so I got it black. Cream and sugar are in the bag."

She nodded, uncaring about the donut she held now crushed in her hand. Dylan took one of the coffees for himself and walked away. She watched his fine back before recovering from whatever had just happened.

What *had* just happened? He'd kissed her again and just as quickly ended it.

She didn't know what to think of the man and definitely couldn't process how he made her feel. Not just his kisses but even the act of giving her breakfast made her feel special and cared for. She'd been on her own for a lot of years, and human kindness or connection wasn't something she'd experienced since the death of her mother and then her father within the same year. More than once since their passing, she'd thought of how nice it would be to have someone take care of her again, even if it was just making her dinner.

Dylan had done that and more.

But no, she was just a job to him. All these things she was thinking and feeling were false. She couldn't even trust herself right now.

* * * * *

Dammit, why had he kissed her again? He'd given into his baser instincts and claimed those plump lips for his own, and now he had a raging boner as well as a crack in his conscience.

She was under his charge, and the last thing he wanted was for her to believe he was taking advantage of her.

Automatically, he took a sip of the coffee he held but tasted nothing but that sweet woman standing not far away, trying to appear busy. But he could tell by the set of her spine that she was as affected by their kiss as he was.

Hell.

He watched her for another minute and then Chaz got his attention. "All finished and just in time. I'm going to head out of here before the streets start filling up for celebrations. Mind if I take one of those donuts?"

"No, go ahead," he said absently.

Chaz walked over to the donut bag and took one fat ring. Then he said something quietly to Athena.

She turned to glance at Dylan, and his gut tightened painfully. Son of a bitch, he hadn't felt this way about anyone since the seventh grade when he'd get butterflies each time Mandy Harkness would glance at him in study hall. He'd never admitted that to his brothers, not wanting to be teased or for one of them to go over his head and ask her out on Dylan's behalf.

He hoped to hell Chaz wasn't doing that with Athena now.

Will you go out with my brother Y or N?

He cut off a groan. Chaz said something else that brought a small smile to the edges of Athena's lips. Dylan focused on her eyes, though, and they looked like flint—dark with anger and annoyance. And why shouldn't she feel those things? Knight Ops had torn apart her life and her boutique and then ordered her to restore it all in the same twenty-four hours.

Chaz took his leave with a chin lift of goodbye to Dylan, and he returned it. The team mantra filled his head: *Guts and glory.* Besides words to live by, the saying had become a greeting or farewell, depending on occasion.

Dylan and Athena exchanged a look. They were alone.

That roused deep pangs in his groin. Getting her against the wall or over that counter—

"Don't you have something to hook up or a screen to watch?" Her snappish tone slammed him, and he suddenly wished things were much different. That he could have met her on different terms—at a Mardi Gras party or at the coffeeshop. Then he wouldn't be the enemy and she wouldn't be off limits.

Since the last of his team had left the shop, the air seemed charged.

Athena was right—he couldn't stand around staring at her this way. It wasn't doing either of them any good, and the zipper on his jeans was in jeopardy.

Turning, he walked into the office.

The place smelled like her perfume but otherwise was devoid of her personal touches. No photos, no vases of flowers.

While he knew her story from researching her background, those details did not spell out a personality. What did she like?

One of his brothers had righted the closet and fixed the door. When he pulled it open, he saw her shoe there—only one—like Cinderella's left behind at the ball.

He sank to the chair and stared at the monitor. It was split into six squares, and Athena was visible in one. He watched her for a second before feeling like a voyeur. But Ben had also reminded him that they'd come to this boutique believing her part of the terrorist ring, and while Ben himself didn't buy it, Athena *was* in contact with the people they were watching.

Dylan rubbed at the bite mark on his palm for a moment. The hours were quickly slipping by and she was not prepared to open Athena's Creations.

He could walk into the showroom and speak to her or he could play with his new toys.

He pressed a button and spoke quietly into the mic hidden at the neck of his shirt. "Athena."

"Jesus Christ!" Her cry echoed, and she whirled to glare at the nearest concealed camera.

Under any other circumstances, he'd get a thrill out of teasing her into a state of annoyance and then cajoling her right out of it.

And then out of her skirt.

"You can't just speak to me out of nowhere like God or something. What do you want, Knight?"

A small thrill ran through him at her use of his last name. For some reason, the toughness in her voice combined with the throatiness sent his libido into overdrive.

"I think you should clean up and at least get some shoes on. Plus, there are those alterations for Landrenau to complete."

She moved closer to the camera until he could see the angry lights flickering in her dark eyes. She raised both hands and flipped him a double bird.

Laughing now, he sat back and fiddled with some settings while she walked over to a bar and ripped a dress off it. She went into the dressing room and when she came out, he gaped at the screen. In color HD, it was as good a view as he'd get of her curves rocking a red dress. She stormed to the shoe wall she'd just spent over an hour working on and pulled down some heels.

While she slipped her feet into these, she bundled all her hair into a knot on the back of her head and took some accessories from a display to hold the mass.

What he wouldn't give to pluck those slender sticks from her curls and let her silky hair fall into his hands.

Right before he captured her mouth.

And wedged his knee high against her pussy again.

Fucking hell, he wished his brothers hadn't barged into the safe house and had let him finish jacking off.

Something onscreen caught his eye, and he tore his gaze from Athena to the square centered on the front door of the shop.

Shit.

He scooted to the edge of his seat and spoke to her via the intercom. "There's someone coming to the door."

She whirled to look. "I don't open for another half hour."

"Do you know this woman?"

"Yes, she's a client."

"The one who wanted the jeweled shoes?"

"No," she said tersely.

He pressed another button to alert Roades, who was on standby in the alley behind the boutique, watching the exterior of the building.

Dylan spoke to Athena again. "Smile, act natural and let her in."

For the next thirty minutes, he analyzed Athena's every move, and she didn't give a single indication that she was doing anything but selling pretty dresses to the woman. Something like relief snaked through Dylan. His instincts had only told him to take her with him, and he was certain it was to keep her safe, not keep her under house arrest.

After the client apologized for the third time for coming by the boutique so early because she was in a hurry to wrap up her errands, Athena checked the woman out and then saw her to the door.

That was where Roades came in. "Tail her," Dylan commanded.

"With my ninja stealth." Roades' joke had Dylan snorting. They'd taken to calling their youngest team member Ninja after the motorcycle he rode.

Athena went to a tall closet and drew out another gown in a bag. She hung it on a hook and then got on her hands and knees, showing off her round backside in the red dress, and began to hem it.

He watched her for an hour before she got another customer. After that, the boutique flooded with people coming for their Mardi Gras clothing, and Athena was hopping. He could also see she was in her element—she loved this as much as he loved his job.

Except at times like this, he wished he wasn't on the receiving end of her ire, that he was just a man and her a woman.

His phone buzzed, and he glanced at the screen. One of his brothers. He picked up.

"It's Roades. Dude, you fucking owe me one."

"For what?"

"Tailing that woman. Gawd." He made a disgusted noise in the back of his throat. "Man, I had to follow her to the nail place and watch her get her feet done. You can't imagine the fucking horrors that are her bunions. Woman needs plastic surgery or some shit."

Dylan had been so strained for so many hours that his brother's words had him outright laughing.

"You think this is funny? I'm not kidding about you owing me one."

"Anything—I'll do anything."

"Then you can hook me up with the sister of that friend of yours."

"Margot's sister?"

"Uh-huh. I want the full date—dinner, show, and you're buying the tickets, too—and dessert."

"I don't know if I can get her to agree to the dessert you're referring to."

"No, I'll take care of that with my own charm and wit. Just get me in the door."

"Fine. I'll even buy you a six-pack to erase the memory of those bunions."

"Dear God."

Dylan laughed again. "Okay, I've got another person for you to tail so get your ass back here. I'll have Athena hold him until you arrive."

Chapter Five

"I've got to get Athena back to the safe house. She's dead on her feet."

Athena paused outside the office door at the sound of Dylan's words as he spoke on the phone. He gave an answering grunt to the person on the other end of the line.

She held her breath, listening. Her parents had taught her not to eavesdrop, but she was pretty sure if they were alive, they'd make a contingency clause that said if she was being held against her will, she was allowed to listen in about what would happen to her next.

Her body felt weighted and her eyes grainy. She couldn't argue part of what Dylan had said—she felt about to hit the floor and pass out from exhaustion. At her busiest time of year, she'd served all those clients on no sleep.

But she *would* fight about going to the safe house. If he didn't realize she wasn't a threat by now, then his skull was thicker than she'd guessed.

"I'll keep you posted," Dylan said as he wrapped up.

Taking a deep breath, Athena popped around the doorframe and her hand fluttered to her chest.

Her office was no longer hers but a high-tech military surveillance station.

All words died on her lips as she gazed around her. "What have you done to my office?" She scrubbed a hand over her face, feeling the skin stretch in unflattering ways.

Dylan stood and rounded the desk, dismissing her question. "Are you ready to go? All finished here for the day?"

She shook her head. "Can't I just go home? Surely you saw what you came here to see." Standing amidst the monitors and listening devices and God knew what else Dylan was using, she felt like she'd been dropped into a TV spy show. That left her feeling more unreal.

He rested a warm hand on her shoulder, and she twitched under his touch. The contact was doing unspeakable things to her insides.

"Athena, do you have anybody close to you that would be placed in danger if the suspects found out about them?"

Her jaw fell open. "You mean you don't already know the name of the clerk at the convenience store that rang out my order? And that I bought a sweet tea and some potato chips to satisfy a salt craving?"

He let go of her shoulder as if singed by her words. Good, let him know the worst side of her, this sleep-deprived, frightened part of her that was furious at feeling she had absolutely no control or say in her life anymore.

"Athena, we can't know everything. Besides, I figured you for a sweet cravings girl."

"I'm having a nightmare and can't wake up." She scrubbed at her face again, about to topple forward and sleep face-down on the carpet under her desk.

"Please answer me." Why were his eyes so warm? Better yet, why did she even notice?

"No, I don't have anyone special. Now that you know I'm a sad thirty-something who's all alone in the world and lives to create and sell clothes to people with too much money, are you happy with yourself?"

"No." He pitched his voice low, and her insides, already mush, flowed with honey.

"Well, I'm going home now. Same time tomorrow?" She started past him.

He caught her elbow, swinging her back. So close. Why was he looming over her this way, like he was going to kiss her again?

"I can't let you leave alone. You know you have to come with me to the safe house for another night."

Another hot, sticky night filled with storms and him sitting outside her door, waiting to catch her in his solid arms when she tripped over him? Or to make her a snack to take her mind off the situation?

Or to pin her to the wall and capture her lips with such dark passion that she still hadn't fully recovered?

She felt her jaw lift a notch as she looked at him. He stared back, some of the concern etched around his eyes replaced by amusement.

"Are you laughing at me?"

"Not at all, Athena. You're a very strong woman, and that pleases me."

"I—" She snapped her mouth shut. What did she say to that?

A shivery sigh left her, and a warmth she didn't want to acknowledge lodged low in her belly.

He kneaded her shoulder, sending sparks down through her torso that somehow tugged hard on her nipples.

She should step back.

She couldn't step back—she was pinned in his intense stare, the same stare that held her in place right before he'd kissed her.

His chest heaved and she felt a shudder move through him.

Suddenly, he let her go, and she rocked on her heels. "I need to take you to the safe house," he said gruffly.

She wanted to argue, but was there any point? She hadn't gotten her way at any time with this hardened special ops man and likely never would.

She sighed. "Fine." At least there was a bed.

He studied her closer as if her agreement stunned him. But he nodded and waved a hand for her to exit the office first. She set about the motions to close her boutique, shutting off lights, locking the register and stuffing all the cash into an envelope she slipped into her purse.

"Stuffing them in your pantyhose would be safer. That's how you transport your cash?" He looked about to have a stroke.

"Yes, why?"

"In this city? Hell, in any city?"

"I've never had a problem, Dylan."

"Until you're mugged or worse for a few thousand in cash."

Ignoring his dark warnings, she tightened her hold on her purse and walked to the back door. When she opened it, a scream bubbled in her throat at the sight of a huge man dressed in all black.

"Sorry, Miss Athena. It's just me." Roades gave her what seemed to be a nod trademarked among all the Knight Ops men. They must practice it in front of a mirror to perfect the move.

"Any updates?" Dylan asked his brother.

"*Nada.* We good here?"

It was Dylan's turn to give that nod. Only on him, it was sooo much sexier. She twisted her gaze away.

"See ya at O-500 then," Roades said.

Five? Who was getting up at five and whatever for? She had no intention of peeling her eyes open before seven and still having plenty of time to open her boutique at eight-thirty.

She started to step out the door, but Dylan grabbed her by the shoulder and shoved her behind him. She glared at his muscled back while he scouted the alley as if ISIS was lying in wait for them.

She followed the line of his arm down to his hand which rested at the waistband at his back. With the thick muscles on either side of his spine, she couldn't detect the bulge of a weapon but knew he had his hand on it.

"Is this really necessary? Isn't Roades out here to keep anybody from being in the alley waiting to attack us?" She went on tiptoe to see over his shoulder, but all she did was bring her nose closer to the cotton of his shirt. The pine-and-musk-scented cotton.

He relaxed. "Sorry, it's habit."

Finding no Kung Fu fighters, men with chains or snipers in the alley behind her boutique, he stepped outside. He reached back and clasped his fingers over her forearm, and she gulped at the heat penetrating her flesh. Too well she recalled the feel of him pinned to her as they kissed.

This was insanity. She had to find a way to disentangle her confused emotions from this man who was nothing more than a glorified bodyguard trained by the US military.

When he drew her outside, he positioned his body in a way that spoke of taking bullets for her. And damn if that wasn't sexy as hell too.

No, no, no. She had to shut down these thoughts. Her mind was too hazy, not working right without a solid eight hours of rest.

Taking her to the vehicle parked at the end of the alley, his head swiveled right and left as he put her inside.

"With all these security measures, I might as well be the First Lady."

He didn't even crack a smile, his expression as stern as ever. The man really had no sense of humor. He got behind the wheel and started the car. They rolled out of the alley and into the street.

They didn't go two blocks before they hit the heart of the Mardi Gras celebrations. She blinked at the bright lights and fireworks being set off. People swarmed the sidewalk and streets, and heavy security barely held them in check.

She gave a sigh.

"What is it?" he asked, eyes darker in the dimness of the car.

"I love this time of year. From my apartment, I have access to so many festivities." A deep longing for her own sacred space rose up in her.

"I can't take you there, Athena."

She turned her head to look at him, a challenge in her voice. "Why? If you're so great at your job, shouldn't you have realized by now that I'm not the person you're looking for and have no connection to terrorism?"

He had to draw to a stop to allow a throng of people to cross the street, each dressed in feathers, hats or wearing glow in the dark necklaces.

"My only job right now is to watch over you."

"You mean watch me."

"Watch over," he repeated, lips hardened.

"I don't understand why you'd believe I'm in danger if that's the story you're sticking with." She folded her arms across her chest, suddenly chilled.

"Have you considered that anybody can find out your apartment address just by doing a little digging, Athena? Or follow you on the bus or in a cab? It isn't safe, and I won't risk you."

His deep voice threaded through her body, leaving her coated in a dew of perspiration. Great, now her body was premenopausal, cold one minute and hot the next. It had nothing to do with the hunk of a man beside her, steering them expertly through the crowded streets and willing to whip out his gun and have a shootout to protect her.

She crossed her legs, and he glanced over, tracking the movement. She squeezed her thighs together harder and tried not to think of that kiss.

Soon, though, exhaustion crept over her, and lulled by the movement of the car, she drifted off.

When a touch on her shoulder startled her awake, she looked up into Dylan's face.

Something moved behind his eyes. "We're here. Come on."

She climbed out, foggy-brained and wanting nothing but a bed. Hell, at this point, she'd take a blanket on the floor. She just needed sleep.

He opened the front door using a passcode and a key card. Then he switched on a light and paced through the house, probably checking it for intruders.

When he returned, she took one look at his serious expression and let out a giggle.

He cocked his head, his own smile playing around the corners of his hard lips. "What's funny?"

"We're in a safe house yet you're checking for dangers."

He grunted his amusement. "Can't be too safe. Can I fix you some dinner or—?

She waved him away. "Bed. That's all I want."

The thunder was already rolling in, the humidity bringing the storms all week. It made for unhappy Mardi Gras revelers and street vendors who made most of their year's income off this one celebration.

She hardly registered her own footsteps as she headed to the bedroom. She pushed open the door, walked straight to the bed and collapsed face down. Her eyes slammed shut, and she was already breathing the deep inhalations of sleep.

97

Seconds later, she felt Dylan removing her shoes and then a light blanket covering her. She snuggled down and everything vanished except the knowledge of his presence.

* * * * *

He woke immediately, heart jerking against his ribs as the click of a door opening hit his senses. He was on his feet, hand on his weapon, when he realized Athena stood over him, eyes wide and blurred from sleep.

He rubbed his hand over his face. "You all right?"

"The storm woke me."

"How about that hot chocolate again?"

She nodded, and his heart gave a new kind of lurch. One that told him he was getting in over his head with this woman.

Feeling rumpled from sleeping in front of her door, he made his way to the kitchen. When he reached into the fridge for milk, he saw it was restocked after Knight Ops had looted it earlier. As he retrieved a small cooking pot and the ingredients he needed, Athena took a seat on the stool again.

Lightning streaked outside, brightening the room enough that he could see her watching him.

"The storm will have driven all the festivities indoors," she said softly.

"Lots to do indoors to celebrate." He poured milk into the pot and added sugar, cocoa powder and a dash of vanilla and then set the pot on the gas burner.

"That's my mother's recipe too."

He smiled. "Probably the recipe of mothers everywhere, considering it's written on the back of the cocoa can." He held it up and she gave a soft laugh. Everything about her was soft and feminine to the extreme. She still wore the red dress, and he wished to hell he'd thought to have clothes brought for her.

He'd have to figure something out because they were in it for the long haul. Knight Ops was staked out on the boutique until they pinpointed the suspect. They had the contacts of Athena's regular clients and were digging into their backgrounds. But Dylan secretly hoped nothing was unearthed right away — he was enjoying being close to this woman far too much.

He set a mug of cocoa in front of her, and she wrapped her fingers around it. "I have a request, Dylan."

His heart picked up at her use of his name.

She went on, "I'd like a shower—in my own shower with my own things. And I want to wear my own clothes, not inventory from my store."

Lightning streaked down again, bringing her into sharper focus. Her face was calm, but he saw how tightly she held her mug, as if anticipating his refusal.

He stared at her for a long moment. "We'll go after we finish this." He lifted his own mug and sipped. The chocolate hit his tongue, but his mind was so fixated on Athena that he could only taste her.

She took three sips and then hopped off the stool. "I'll get my shoes."

He watched her hips twitch out of the kitchen and set the mug down a bit too hard. Dammit, he needed to get his mind off having her and stick to the mission.

But his body was telling him that his full-time job should be running his hands up and down her body, slanting his mouth across hers and then sliding his cock deep inside her just to hear her soft sighs of pleasure.

After only a minute, she returned. "The rain's slowed down. If we hurry, we can run through the raindrops."

He smiled at her expression, something his *maman* used.

"I'm ready," he said.

In the car, she started to give him directions to her place, but he knew where she lived—knew everything about her.

Everything except how she liked to be made love to.

He bit off a groan as he drew up in front of her apartment building. The streets empty of crowds, all driven inside by the storm, and the pavement was inky black with rain, reflecting streetlights. He looked to her. "Stay here while I check things out."

He expected her argument, but she only nodded.

Thrown off balance by her lack of sass on the matter, he got out of the car and scanned the surroundings. He didn't trust her not to leave the car while he went inside and looked around, so he opened her door.

She slipped out and followed him to the front door. He unlocked it, and she let out a soft gasp, a rasp that shot need through his groin.

"You took my key."

"This is a universal key. Works on every lock I've ever encountered."

"Well, that isn't unnerving," she muttered.

He smiled as he entered first, keeping a hand on her arm and blocking her with his body. "Stay here." He went into stealth mode. In a minute flat, he'd searched every closet and corner of her apartment. He came back to stand before her. "All clear."

She gave him an are-you-kidding-me stare.

"Why didn't you just turn on the lights and look around instead of skulking through the dark? You're your biggest fan, aren't you?" She leaned over and switched on a lamp on a table next to the door.

In the ring of light, he studied her, taken aback once again by her beauty. That little mark above her lip made him burn to drag her close and kiss her until she melted under his touch.

She moved into the space, turning on another lamp, and he turned to watch her. Her place was filled with ethnic details—a South American hand-loomed rug, embroidered pillows from Istanbul, a piece of hand-thrown pottery from Morocco.

"You travel," he said.

Her gaze flew to his. She nodded. "Once a year I travel to a new destination to find new and special fashions and textiles."

He stepped up to the sofa and touched a pillow. "I was in Turkey and saw fabrics just like this in the marketplace."

She moved to stand next to him. "You travel too then."

His gaze landed on her, and damn if his heart didn't kick into an erratic beat. His breath came faster too, but he was a sniper and knew how to control his responses.

"Go take your shower and pack. I'll wait here."

She seemed to hesitate a moment longer before turning and disappearing into the bedroom.

He dropped like a stone to the sofa, head in hands. Visions of her bed, plush with extravagant findings from around the world and inviting as hell, loomed behind his eyes. Fuck, how was he ever going to keep from walking into that bathroom and stripping down to shower with her? Soaping her all over?

Damn. He had to do something to distract himself from thoughts of her completely naked in the other room.

He texted Chaz. *What's up tonight?*

No reply came and after ten minutes, Dylan gave up. His brother was probably getting lucky while he sat here in torment.

The shower shut off and that launched him into another level of torture. He pushed to his feet and started pacing, counting each step. When that didn't distract him enough, he counted in Spanish, French and Russian. Then did it backward.

A curse sounded from the bedroom, and he stopped mid-pace, the hackles on his neck standing up.

Athena let out another curse, and he rushed to the bedroom. At the door, he froze, taking in the situation.

She sat on the edge of the bed in nothing but a thick white towel, her hair wrapped in a smaller white towel. And she was holding a tissue to her leg.

"Blood. I smell blood." He hit his knees before her and grabbed the tissue. When he drew it away, he saw a simple shaving cut trickling with blood.

"It's nothing—I just cut myself shaving and didn't notice until now. H-how do you smell blood?"

He gently swabbed at the cut, applying pressure just like he did to his jaw when he sliced himself. "I'll stop the bleeding and then you can tell me where the bandages are."

God, her calf was perfectly formed, the muscle toned. Under his hand, her skin was scorching hot and moist from her shower.

His cock bulged.

"Dylan?"

He looked up her body, tearing his gaze from her terrycloth-covered thighs and what was beneath. He swallowed hard. "Yes?"

"How can you smell blood?" Her eyes were luminous. It was the middle of the night, and she was still working on little sleep. He shouldn't be thinking of why his cock twitching at the look she was giving him.

"When you've seen battle, you learn the smell pretty quick."

She bit down on her lower lip, depressing all that plump flesh.

He couldn't take it anymore.

He cupped her face and surged upward to claim her mouth. The soft gasp she made spiked his need higher, and he took control. Plunging his tongue deeper, tasting fresh toothpaste and pure woman. She shivered and then touched her tongue tentatively to his.

Oh fuck. I'm a goner.

The shaving cut forgotten, he closed his hands over her waist, learning how small she felt all over again as he plundered her mouth.

"Dylan." Her whisper seared through him, and it took everything he had to pull away. Panting, he tried to form an apology, but all that filled his mind was a series of commands.

Lie back. Pull down that towel so I can look at your beautiful body.

Spread your thighs.

He jammed his fingers into his hair.

"What is it, *cher*?" His voice was so gritty, he might as well be in the thick of chemical warfare.

"I…" She stopped, chewing her plump lower lip again.

He was a patient man, but hell if he wanted to wait for her to tell him to leave her alone and to find someone who had better control to watch over her.

She lifted her fingers to the top of her towel, snug over her breasts, and tugged out the corner. When she parted the cloth to reveal her very curvy, very bare body, she watched his face.

A rough noise escaped him. "Jesus, Athena."

She glanced up at him shyly. "I want you, Dylan. I like how you kiss me, and you make me feel…" She struggled to finish the sentence.

"I know how you feel." He growled as he laid hands on her. Bare shoulders, across her collarbones and down to her breasts. Strumming each perky nipple with a forefinger before circling and making them pucker.

She tossed her head back, and the towel fell off. Her wet hair tumbled down.

He watched her face as he continued to explore, cupping each breast in a palm, dizzied by the soft weights. His cock throbbed in time to his racing heart.

As he skimmed his hands down her torso to the flare of her hips, she moaned. His gaze latched on to the trim patch of dark hair on her mound. He groaned—fuck, he'd wanted to thrust his tongue into her slick folds since first setting eyes on her. All Knights loved eating pussy, or so his brothers claimed, and Dylan was no different.

Athena lay back on the bed, arms flung upward in surrender. Was she really going to give herself to him this way? Fuck, he didn't deserve her.

He stretched his fingers across her round thighs and caressed all the way down to her knees. He checked the cut with a glance and found it had stopped bleeding. Then he was moving his hands up her body once more, touching every spot he'd missed while her breaths came in small pants.

He hovered over her, gazing deep into her eyes. "You're certain?"

She nodded and slipped a hand around his nape to draw him down for a kiss. The moment their mouths connected, his body took over. Hands roving,

106

plucking at her nipples before he eased his lips down to close around the hard tip.

She cried out, hooking one ankle around his body. The move brought the rich scents of her arousal and clean woman to him, and that was it.

He jerked his head up to meet her stare. "I have to taste you, *cher*. Now."

* * * * *

She barely registered what Dylan meant before he scraped his stubbled jaw down her belly and spread her thighs wide. Without hesitating, he buried his face in her pussy.

"Oh my God!" Her voice wobbled as he parted his mouth over her slick sex. Extreme warmth claimed her. He kissed her pussy gently, up and down the seam and then across her clit once, twice...

She stiffened with each pass. At this rate, she'd be coming apart in seconds, but she wanted it to last so long.

"Mmm. You taste like heaven." His eyes flashed before he thumbed apart her folds and he sank his tongue into her pussy.

Liquid need flowed through her like lava, and she lifted her hips off the bed to meet each tongue thrust. Passion took hold. He tongued her in and out until her inner thighs shook and then he moved up to close his lips around her aching nubbin.

Electricity rained down on her, and she felt she was part of the electrical storm from earlier—or maybe it was still going on outside, she had no clue. She was too deep in Dylan to even care if the whole building exploded around them.

He sucked on her clit until she stopped breathing. Then he sank one finger inside her channel. Her inner muscles clamped on the digit, and he gave a moan.

"I need to touch you. Take off your clothes," she pleaded.

"Not yet." His words whispered across her wet pussy. "I'm not finished with you." With that, he dived back in, licking, lapping and caressing until her hips bucked and she thrashed her head.

"I'm close. Please." She dug her fingers into his shoulders.

He doubled his efforts, swirling his tongue around her clit and thrusting two fingers inside her. Stars burst behind her eyes, and she quivered, hanging on the edge of an abyss. When the first contraction hit, she screamed. Waves pounded her hard and fast, and she couldn't even suck in enough air as he teased more pulsations out of her.

Long minutes passed, and he slowed his movements, pulling more moans from her lips. Then he sucked her clit hard and stretched her pussy with three fingers, leaving her aching for more.

For his cock.

"Dylan." Her voice was a plea.

He moved up her body, kissing each inch of skin in his path. When he reached her lips, he looked down into her eyes. "I'm going to share your flavors with you." He kissed her. The wetness on his mouth was salty-sweet, and she'd never tasted anything so hot before. Thrusting her tongue between his lips, she tugged at his T-shirt. Big, warm muscles were too good to ignore. She ran her hands over his shoulders, chest and back. Each cut and dip tightened that knot of need in her core.

Skating her hand down his washboard abs only left her shaking with need. She went for his belt.

He stayed her hand, holding it in place. Under the cloth, the bulge of his erection told her just how big he was.

"I need your cock inside me."

A grunt that was near pain left him, and he dropped his forehead to hers. "I need to know you want this for real, Athena. Not just because the situation is frightening."

What situation? All she could think of was how much she wanted this man.

She nodded. "I want you."

He paused another heartbeat. "I can't stop once I get inside you."

A shudder of pleasure ran through her. "I don't want you to stop. Hurry, Dylan."

"Jesus." His blasphemy was almost a prayer as he got to his feet and stripped down his cargo pants followed by his briefs. When his thick length bobbed against his hard abs, she stared at the delicious outline. Mushroomed head, swollen to purple and glazed with juices. She wondered if he tasted as good as she tasted to him.

Reaching out, she wrapped her fingers around the base. He stood at the edge of the bed, letting her jack him three times, four. Then he gripped her wrist hard enough to stop her.

"I can't let you touch me." He sounded as if he'd run a marathon carrying three of the men of the Knight Ops team.

"You're so beautiful." She ran her gaze over his muscled body to his thick cock nestled in a patch of hair centered between steely thighs.

"You're the one who's beautiful." He produced a condom from somewhere in his pants and tore it open. Watching him roll it on shouldn't be one of the most erotic things she'd ever seen, but she had a feeling everything this man did took a new height.

When he slid back into bed, he rolled her atop him, planting his hands on her ass and kissing her until she started to wiggle with impatience again.

"Come up here and sit on my face." His rough order made her stomach bottom out with a thrill.

"I've never…"

"Then it's time." He guided her up until her thighs were settled around his ears. He closed his eyes and began to lick her.

* * * * *

Fuck, she was so responsive that he didn't think he'd live through the moment. But he couldn't stop dipping his tongue into her sweet pussy either. Using short flicks across her clit and then pulling her forward so he could plunge his tongue deep again. Need spread through him as she climbed higher toward her release.

Rocking on his face, taking what she needed, she was the most stunning creature he could ever imagine. When the first pulsations struck, his instinct was to hold her there and draw the biggest orgasm of her life from her. But he lifted her off his face, moved her down his body and sank into her still-quivering channel.

She cried out and rocked harder. A grunt left him. Her scorching heat surrounded him, hugged him tight. She slid up and down his shaft, milking him until he felt that deep pressure building at the base of his spine.

Cradling her head, he brought her down to his mouth, and their kiss spiraled on and on. In the distance, a rumble of thunder shook the city. Then another.

She broke the kiss to stare down into his eyes. "Dylan."

She was so close, so tight, so hot, soooo wet.

"Let it come, *cher*. Come for me."

111

She withdrew on his cock once more time, pure bliss crossing her beautiful features as her release hit.

He couldn't watch her pleasure for more than two strokes before his own claimed his senses, ripping a roar from his mouth. Jets of hot cum seared up out of him, and her pussy clenched and released rhythmically.

Oh Jesus, was his first thought.

Then, *Fucking hell.*

He'd had her and too late he realized once would never be enough.

Nothing would be enough — not one long, meaningful look, one stolen kiss, one night.

Athena must have channeled some old voodoo powers of the region because she'd completely, utterly stolen his soul.

* * * * *

It was impossible to feel regret for taking what she wanted from Dylan when her body still felt like warm pudding.

She stretched, nudging his shoulder as she did. With a hand on her back, he drew her against him, and she found a spot on his chest that fit her head perfectly. Under her ear, his heart thundered.

Looking down his body, she drank in the sculpted beauty of muscle stacked on by years of hard physical training. Dark hair sprinkled his chest and ran in a trail down his abs to his cock before spattering his thighs and calves. His feet were long and as manly as the rest of him.

"What's that for?" he rumbled.

"What?"

"You sighed."

"Did I?" She'd have to watch it with this one—she was prone to girly habits she'd avoided before. Even as a teenager, she'd never been boy crazy. Maybe because she'd been holding out for the opportunity to go man crazy.

She sighed.

"You did it again."

She giggled. "I can't seem to help it." She tilted her head to look up at him, and he smiled, smoothing her wild hair with one hand.

"I hope that's the sound of complete pleasure," he said.

"Duh. Did you feel me come three times?"

He stuck out his tongue and wagged it, shooting liquid need between her thighs again. "Definitely felt it." He stopped stroking her hair and walked his fingers down her spine. The soft touch had her squirming for more, and judging by the hardness of his cock, he could go for another round himself.

Flattening her hand on his abs, she smiled when he sucked in sharply. She slipped her hand downward to wrap her fingers around his cock.

"Fuck, Athena."

"That's my intention." Where had all this boldness come from? She wasn't a virgin by any means, but her business had taken up so much of her life in the past few years that she'd forgotten how to be a woman. With Dylan it was easy to remember.

Pushing onto one elbow to watch his face, she gave a test stroke of his cock.

With a groan, he jerked his hips. Every hard inch of his body turned her on. The creases of muscle and tendon in his thighs tugged as he stretched under her hand-strokes. She watched his face shudder with pleasure and a heady thrill ran through her that she could give this to him.

Her own pussy was slick with need, her inner thighs damp.

"Kiss me," he grated out, cupping her nape.

She leaned in to capture his lips, controlling the tempo until she couldn't stand it another minute and moaned. When she parted her lips, he plunged his tongue inside and rolled her so she was pinned beneath him.

Staring up into his eyes, she had another moment where she wondered if any of this was real. Then again, the whole week was turning out to be a confusing mess, and this... *This* felt like the only thing that *was* real since Knight Ops had crashed through her back door.

She looped her arms around his neck, tugging him atop her. Loving the feel of his weight, she kissed back with all the passion he roused inside her. Finally, he tore from the kiss and stared down at her, chest working.

"*Cher*, we have a problem."

"What's that?" Her clouded mind took a second to clear.

"I'm out of condoms."

"Oh. Drawer." She waved at her nightstand.

His eyes narrowed so minutely that she might have missed it if she hadn't been looking closely. "You keep condoms in your nightstand?"

He didn't sound as though he liked the thought of her being prepared to sleep with someone. Or maybe he didn't like the idea of her sleeping with someone besides him.

"Modern women take care of ourselves."

He considered her a minute. "Good thing you do because we special ops guys don't have room to carry more than one." He shot her a crooked grin and leaned to the side to pull open the drawer.

When he pushed to his knees to jerk the rubber over his swollen length, she ran her hands up to her throbbing nipples. He went dead still, watching her.

"You touch yourself?"

"I thought we established I'm a modern woman." She circled each nipple twice before he issued a growl and took over. Clamping his mouth over one breast while pinching the other with a skill that had her on edge.

An invisible knot in her stomach tightened, and her pussy squeezed. He hovered over her, weight braced on his elbows, bathing her breasts with his tongue and grazing the tips with his teeth until she couldn't stand it another second.

She wrapped her thighs around him and jerked him down and into her. He filled her with one quick glide, and they both fell still. His cock stretched her, the head skimming a place so deep, she didn't think any man had found it before.

"Move," she pleaded, rocking into him.

The cords on his neck stood out as he withdrew with insane slowness. His eyes seemed to darken with each inch he pulled out. When he slammed home again, they shared a cry. The room lit with another flash of lightning. Heat enveloped Athena as he tongue-fucked her mouth to the same pace of his cock thrusts.

Her insides gripped at him, never wanting this moment to end. In the light of day, she didn't know how she'd feel about what she'd done. But for now, she was going to tuck away every minute of their coupling and think about Dylan when she was alone later. And she would be alone, because no way would this continue after Knight Ops ended their mission.

He did an erotic pushup over her, sinking deep and holding her captive with his gaze. She dug her nails into his shoulders and rose to meet him. The bed shook, and the Indonesian cutwork-style headboard tapped the wall lightly.

"Fuck, you're beautiful." His rough words shouldn't fill her with extreme warmth, but they did. She'd been told this before by family, friends and many others. But somehow, it was different coming from Dylan's hard lips.

She arched up to kiss him, feeding him her moans as the rhythm of his movements began to grow more disjointed. His cock swelled within her, and her pussy clenched. A pulse began deep in her core.

"Oh God, I'm so close." She threw her head back, and he latched onto her neck, kissing and nibbling as he ground his cock into her.

He slid his hand between their bodies and using a callused fingertip, pressed down on her clit.

She exploded in a wave of ecstasy, stars bursting behind her closed eyes — or maybe that was the lightning. Her own breaths sobbed in her hearing.

"Open your eyes. Look at me, *cher*."

His command made her eyes pop open. She stared up into the glassy depths of his gaze. He grimaced in pleasure and stiffened. When he growled out his release, fucking her furiously, she held onto him, riding out the last of her own orgasm.

She came to her senses to find the covers over her and Dylan gone. Quickly, she pushed to her elbows and saw the glimmer of the bathroom light. She collapsed back to the pillow — her own fluffy cloud of a pillow, feeling the effects of little sleep over the past few days.

Her eyes slipped shut but her mind worked too fast for rest.

When the bed dipped under her, she opened her eyes. Dylan stood there in the buff, his muscled form outlined by the dim glow of streetlights outside the bedroom windows. He climbed into bed, his weight causing her to roll into his arms.

Okay, maybe she wanted to as well.

He tucked her against his chest, one hand protectively on the back of her head. He brushed a kiss between her brows. "That's some bathroom."

She felt herself smile against him. She was really proud of what she'd done in there with paint and updates that went against her rental agreement. But she didn't care.

"I visited—"

"The baths in Budapest?" he filled in.

She started, looking at him hard. "Why, yes. Have you been there?"

He grinned, the corner of his lips tipping in that bad-boy way that started a low flutter in her belly again. "I travel when I get leave."

"I'm impressed."

"The golden walls and stone really capture the feeling of the baths."

"Thank you."

"Your taste in everything is exquisite."

Shyness came over her. Again, people had complimented her this way before but when Dylan said it, she felt like he was peeling back a layer of her skin and seeing things others did not.

"Tell me about those wedding rings you had in your wall safe."

His question took her by surprise. Leaning away to look at him, she said, "What do you want to know? They were my parents'."

"I guess I'm wondering why a shoe with gems worth a quarter million dollars would be in a locked file drawer while rings worth about fifty bucks in gold is kept in a safe."

She stiffened and sat up. "I don't know if I like your tone *or* your question."

He watched her. "Athena—"

"It sounds as if you're accusing me of something. I thought we were beyond that, but I guess not." She swung her legs over the side of the mattress and her toes grazed the thick Persian carpet. She dragged the sheet off the bed, off Dylan, and shielded her nudity from him.

He sat up, unfazed by his nakedness or her anger.

"Yes, Dylan," sarcasm dripped from her, "those wedding bands belong to the head of ISIS and his wife. He's coming back for them at the end of the week and didn't you know that there's a button melted into the gold that when pressed, will blow Louisiana off the map?"

119

Dylan sat up, an expression on his face that she couldn't understand and at the moment, didn't want to. She just wanted him to leave her apartment and get out of her life.

He ran a hand over his face and up to his hair. Dammit, now he looked like a lost little boy with that sadness in his eyes.

He got up and came to her. "Athena, I'm not accusing you of anything."

"You didn't sleep with me to make me tell you my secrets? Secrets I don't have?"

He jerked as if she'd slapped him. "My God, you think I'd do that?"

"I don't know what you'd do. You're a stranger to me."

"I think we're a hell of a lot more than strangers after what we shared." His tone rang with irritation.

She could cave in and cuddle against his broad chest like she wanted to. Or she could stand her ground and force him to see reason when it came to the situation—or get out.

Clutching the sheet to her chest, she stared at him. "I wish I knew what to believe when it comes to you, Dylan. But the fact is, you're either investigating me or protecting me and—"

He gripped her shoulders, pulling her onto tiptoe, his mouth hovering over hers. His heated breath washed over her lips and his eyes burned with intensity. "This world is complicated, Athena. There's a lot I can't tell you, about people who'd try to use you or set you up to take the fall for them." His throat worked as if he choked on the words he wanted to spew. "Fuck it—those shoes with the gems? They're a key piece to what we're after."

"How so?"

He stared into her eyes and finally gave a shake of his head. "I've said too much already. But just know that I'm here for you—to keep you safe and to..." He trailed off, his grip on her changing, softening.

He pulled her against him, molding her to fit his hard chest, her hips nestled to his. A soft noise left her, and she rested her head against his pec.

She must be more exhausted than she thought.

He held her a long minute and then pushed out a sigh. "I've gotta take you back to the safe house. Hell... what I wouldn't do to stay the night here with you."

Chapter Six

"Talk to you a sec?" Ben closed the door of the office where Dylan had set up to monitor all the activity of Athena's Creations.

He gave a nod and looked away from the monitors. For the moment, Athena was alone in the boutique, busy steaming the wrinkles out of a gown.

Ben didn't immediately speak but stared at him.

"What?" Dylan asked.

"Fuck. I don't know why I didn't see it before."

"See what?"

"You're into that woman."

Dylan shook his head. "I'm in charge of her."

"But you get the same look Sean does when he looks at Elise."

Dylan shot his brother and commander a flat look. "This one?"

"No, dumb ass. But never mind—I'm here for another reason."

He sat up straighter, his brother's observations put on the backburner.

"You were right about there being more gems than the ones in those shoes. Roades tracked down the supplier and was told that twelve in total were sold to the buyer."

"Roades tracked him down? Since when is he taking on such sensitive work?"

"Our youngest brother's grown up a lot since joining Knight Ops, bro. He isn't all about shooting 'em up and reloading as fast as he can."

"He's still all about the fucking every pretty girl on his down time that he can, though, right?"

Ben chuckled. "Yeah, that's the same."

Dylan blew out a breath. "Whew. I was scared for a minute. Can't have these guys growing up and settling down too much."

Ben cocked a brow. "What about you? Experiencing any feelings of settling down?"

"Stick to the intel. Was I right about the gems? That there are microchips embedded in them? How many chips did you find?"

"Sean and Elise took out six. She's busy decoding them now."

"So that leaves six in the wind. Do we need to search the shop again?"

"My thought is to have her place another order with the same supplier."

"Athena won't be happy about that."

His brother gazed at him. "Damn, I knew it."

"Quit trying to read more into this than there is." Only, Ben's radar was never wrong, and this was no

123

different. If his brother's alarms were blaring that Dylan was slowly falling for Athena, then he was spot on.

Although after last night, Dylan thought falling for wasn't exactly the right word—he'd *fallen*. Pure and simple, he wanted her. And as soon as he figured out how to get her out of this wreck of a situation, he was going to whisk her away to the family cabin in the bayou, away from obligations and terrorists and spend time learning everything there was to know about her.

"I'll have her pack up all the jewelry and hand it off to Chaz when he gets back from following that banker's wife. But I want you to tell Roades and Sean to look for more than the chips embedded in the jewels."

"Okay?"

"I want them to consider the jewels themselves. Some might be worth more than others—some will be nothing but glass. You may need to bring in an expert on the case and see if any are real. A fat ruby or emerald would be worth enough money to grease the palm of someone influential."

Ben nodded. "This is above our pay grade, but I think your hunch is right. I'll inform Jackson this is our agenda and I'll let you know what we find."

Dylan sat back in the chair, his gaze drifting to the monitor again. His earpiece hummed with a soft tune—Athena was humming.

Ben laughed and shook his head. "Yup, smitten. You're in deep shit, Dylan. Falling for a woman you're either watching or protecting is never going to end well."

"Shut the hell up, Ben. Don't you have a job to do?" He ignored his brother, but his words lingered long after Ben left. He was probably right—about everything. Athena would never see him as a normal guy, a love interest. Not when he was keeping an eye on every move she made and ticking her off with questions about what she kept in her safe.

None of this would end well for him either. He'd already established in his mind that he wanted her.

He grunted. "Too fucking late."

* * * * *

Athena saw the customer out the door with a wave and smile. Humming one of the jaunty Mardi Gras tunes she'd heard blasting from the street festivities, she walked into the dressing room to clean up after the customer.

Gowns were haphazardly hung on the hangers, but Athena wasn't fussed—it was part of her job. She enjoyed helping these clients and seeing smiles on their faces when they walked out feeling so good about their appearances.

She slid the zipper up on one gown and then hooked the shoulder strap more securely on the hanger. She set the gown aside and reached for

125

another. The red dress was exactly what everybody was looking for when it came to Mardi Gras season — there weren't enough sequins or feathers to satisfy a woman going to a good party. In fact, if Athena had to choose, she'd probably select this gown.

She held it up to her curves, imagining the fit on her body. Hugging her breasts and hips and dipping in all the right places.

She pictured how Dylan's eyes would widen when he saw her and how he'd look himself. She'd only ever seen him... Well, in and out of cargo pants. She had no idea if he liked dressing up, but she'd overheard him and one of his brothers talking about catfishing at a cabin in the bayou, and she could easily envision him in that setting. Kicked back in a lawn chair, a beer at his elbow and a rod in hand. His well-worn shorts and T-shirt would fit his muscular body to perfection.

She shivered at the warmth that brought to the surface of her skin. Their night together was something out of a book or movie. He was so attentive and thorough...

She hugged the gown to herself and glanced up and down her reflection.

A breath trickled from her, strangled. The small black speck clinging to the corner of the mirror was unmistakably out of place.

The dress fell from her grasp to puddle on the carpet and she bent to pluck the device off the mirror. Disgust and fury rose up, her chest burning with it. A scream built in her lungs, but she couldn't release it just yet—Dylan deserved every curse that would come from her mouth for what he'd done.

Dress forgotten, she stormed out of the dressing room and crossed the showroom. When she burst into the office, he was typing something into a laptop. He glanced up, and she reeled.

"Since when do you have glasses?" The horn-rimmed frames shouldn't have such effect on her ability to think or the rapid flutter of her heart. But he looked like the sexiest man alive.

A crooked grin tilted the corner of his lips and he eased the glasses off. "They're not for reading."

"Oh." She stared blankly at him, wondering if they were just for making her lose her mind with lust. Then she remembered what she held clutched tightly in her fist and how duplicitous and sneaky this man was.

Her brows lowered, and she strode to his side, thrusting out her open palm. She let him see the device for a moment and then rifled it at his chest.

"You're bugging my dressing rooms now? Is that a camera? You're violating my customers!"

He clapped a hand over the bug before it could fall to his lap. Good thing, because if she looked down and thought about what was behind that zipper of his cargos, all her anger would lose its effect.

He held the device between his long fingers, eyes narrowed.

"I can't tell you how creeped out I am that you'd sink so low, Dylan. I don't care if you're doing it for the government—in fact, that's even worse! Do we have no rights anymore? How about the right to take off our clothes without somebody looking at us on a... a monitor!" She waved at the screens that showed her shop along with a bunch of website tabs on the laptop—apparently he was doing some research on gems.

She opened her mouth to continue telling him off, but his quiet tone stopped her.

"Where did you get this?" He picked at one corner of the device with a thumbnail.

"Haven't you been listening to me? In the dressing room! You put it there or ordered it to be placed there. I still can't bel—"

"This isn't ours."

His words sliced through her like a cold blade of a knife. Her heart tripped, and she slapped a hand to her chest to force it to beat again. All the blood felt like it had run out of her body, leaving her icy.

"What do you mean it isn't yours?" Her words came out reedy because she couldn't find enough oxygen in the same room with Dylan on a good day, and now this?

He leaned over the device, inspecting it closely. Then he snapped to his feet so fast that she stumbled back a step. He put out a hand to catch her, but her

128

back met the wall instead. Thank God, because she needed something solid to hold her up.

If that bug wasn't from Knight Ops, then who?

"When did you notice this?" The urgency in his tone ripped through her.

"I— Just a minute ago when I went into the dressing room to clear it out."

"It wasn't there for the three customers before her?" Of course he had eyes on the last customer and all of those from earlier.

She shook her head, feeling her hair breaking free of the confines of the leather hair band holding it at her nape. Curls swirled around her face. "I don't know. I didn't look that closely before."

"And this time you did?" His arched brows seemed to throw accusations at her. And to think she'd been fantasizing about playing dress-up with him or imagining how he looked in his down time.

"I didn't look at that corner of the mirror before. I'm busy. Dylan, if that isn't yours, whose is it?" Hysteria rang in her voice, and she fought it down. Going off the rails over this wasn't going to help the situation. But she was stressed to the point of meltdown and the only time she hadn't felt attacked by this man was when she was in bed with him. That had been a different kind of attack—one on her senses.

She brushed the curl off her cheekbone, staring at his expression. His emotions were masked, his face far from the animated, gorgeous man she was used to. This guy was a killer, and she remembered thinking how cold and cruel his eyes really were. Fact was, he had multiple sides, and she was just seeing a few of them.

He suddenly hunched over the desk, one thumb rapidly moving over his cell phone while he one-handedly entered some numbers in the keyboard, causing the security footage to flip backward. The hours of the day registered rapidly at the top until he reached the time when the first customer had entered that morning.

Meanwhile, his phone rang faintly. A deep voice answered.

He snatched up the phone and slammed it to his ear. "We've got trouble."

So it was Knight Ops.

She wrapped her arms around herself, feeling all that cold settle into her bones. She couldn't hear the other side of the conversation, only Dylan's words.

"Don't give me any of that Alpha Charlie, Ben. I'm far from distracted from this mission."

Alpha Charlie? She stared at his blank face, seeing none of that warmth she had when rolling around her bed with him.

He sliced a look her way and then returned it to the monitor immediately. "9:43." He flipped forward in the footage. "10:07. And 11:01. Got it? Good—find them and question them."

Athena moved forward and grabbed his arm. "You can't have my clients questioned like common criminals!"

He shook her off, and she stepped back, more stunned by his reaction to her touch than she cared to admit. A pang of hurt stabbed her chest as she realized she was nothing to him but a warm body to get off on. But to her, the previous night had been so much more.

Stupid, she was so stupid.

She started for the door, but Dylan's arm shot out and he snagged her around the chest, the warm steel wrapping her up tight as he drew her back to his chest. With his mouth next to her ear, he spoke to Ben once more.

"See that it's done. You know where to reach me."

She felt him flex when he pocketed his phone. Then he turned her in his hold to look down into her eyes.

"Tell me everything."

"You can see it all—hear it too. What do you think I can possibly tell you that's new?"

His jaw worked as if he was grinding his teeth. She didn't like this cold, hard Dylan. She'd totally let herself fall into the trap of thinking something else might be behind their attraction—that this screwed up relationship could be something more after this nightmare ended.

She'd been a fool.

She pushed away from him and put air between them. Folding her arms, she glared at him. "Stop looking at me like I'm being accused of something. The only thing I'm guilty of is serving my customers and making a sale."

His eyelid twitched and then his mask broke away, leaving the man she recognized standing in front of her. "Athena, someone planted this. It wasn't Knight Ops or any other OFFSUS unit."

He waved a hand sharply through the air. "Look, that device? It can see and hear everything that takes place in that dressing room. It's possible that one woman planted it to pick up intel on the next client or the third. We need to find out—now. And you're in danger. As soon as I get the clear from Chaz, I'm taking you out of here."

"What? I can't leave in the middle of the day. I have appointments, people coming in for wedding tuxes and—"

"Your day is finished."

Her throat closed on whatever she'd been about to say. Besides the cold terror gripping her, was it horrible to think of how damn hot Dylan was when making these decisions about her life?

She must be bonkers, because she liked being in control.

Except when he was stroking her skin, his cock moving inside her...

132

His phone blipped.

"That's Chaz," he said without looking. "Let's go."

"But the money in the register. I take it out every time."

"It's only three hundred dollars. If it's stolen, I'll replace it. We don't have time." He caught her by the hand and dragged her out the office door. He strode too fast for her shorter legs to keep up with and she had to double her pace across the showroom to the back door.

Chaz slipped in, gave his brother a chin nod and then walked to the front door. Out of the corner of her eye, she saw him lock up as Dylan towed her out the back. The vehicle was parked so close to the door that she only had to take one step before she was lifted inside. Dylan's bulk followed her in and then he slammed the door. A second later, Chaz hopped behind the wheel.

The car took off, and she couldn't even focus on the blurs of color flying past the windows. She didn't need to ask to know Dylan was taking her to the safe house. Once again, she felt like someone far more important—a political figure or celebrity facing a threat. But she was just Athena, daughter of hardworking parents, granddaughter of an immigrant who wanted more for his family in America.

She glanced at Dylan from the corner of her eye to see him looking at her feet. She looked down too, wondering what could hold his attention.

He met her gaze. "At least you're wearing shoes this time."

* * * * *

When Athena emerged from the safe house's bedroom, she stopped dead, probably because the whole Knight Ops team was crowded in the living room. They all swung their attention to her, and Dylan pushed down a territorial growl.

Her gaze shifted past each guy as if seeking him. As her eyes met his, a shiver of relief washed over her beautiful features, and dammit, what magic did she have over him?

He stepped forward and took her hand. "Athena, you haven't formally met the guys, but they're setting up here for the time being. That's Ben, Sean, Rocko..." The latter gave her a salute accompanied by a broad smile. "My youngest brother Roades, and you know Chaz."

She nodded to each, but her fingers tightened around Dylan's. The action punched a hole right through him. God, the thought that she'd lean on him... He couldn't imagine how or why he'd been awarded her trust, but it seemed he had it.

"We've brought some pizzas, and we were about to go into the kitchen and eat. Are you hungry?" Dylan asked her.

She shrugged. After the upset back in her store with finding somebody had planted a device in her dressing room, she was shaken.

"C'mon. You guys go ahead but leave me six pieces with sausage and peppers." He led her back into her room and closed the door.

"Six pieces?" she asked.

Okay, maybe she wasn't as stunned as he'd first thought. He grinned. "One thing you learn in my line of work is when there's food, you eat. Maybe you should take my advice." He studied her eyes. "Athena, we're going to find out what happened. I promise you."

"And you're finished thinking I'm the terrorist who planted a device in my own dressing room?"

"I haven't thought that for a while." Actually, today pounded home the belief that she'd become a target. While the thought made him want to grab his rifle and hunt down the bastards responsible, he kept a neutral expression.

"Is this ever going to end?" she asked.

He pushed out a sigh and stepped closer to cup her delicate jaw. "Abso-fucking-lutely. And then—" He cut off, about to say he'd take her home to meet his family. And then on a week-long vacation to Manchu Piccu. He wondered if she'd ever visited the

135

Mayan site, but he'd like to buy her a bunch of textiles for souvenirs.

She lifted a hand to cover his, the slender digits so small in comparison. "Then what?"

He shook his head. He couldn't tell her those things and risk her tucking tail and running. The last thing he wanted was for Athena to feel he was heaping more pressure on her.

"Then you can return to your normal life."

Was that a flicker of disappointment in her eyes? He must be imagining it.

"Are you okay to sit with the guys and eat? If you're uncomfortable—"

"It's okay. I've seen them all before, even if I've only just now formally met them."

"Sorry, you can imagine we have a bad habit of invading a place and not introducing ourselves." He grinned, and she gave a soft chuckle that went straight to his heart. Unable to help himself, he drew her near and brushed his lips across hers. Once, twice. The growl of need was rising inside him, and he had to step back before he threw her on the very close bed and changed the sadness in her eyes to a look of pure bliss.

Stepping back, he slid his hand from her cheek to her shoulder and all the way to her wrist. She turned her hand into his grasp and threaded their fingers. Warmth spread through him.

"Let's see if they saved me that pizza."

In the kitchen, Rocko and Roades had taken over the stools. Ben and Sean leaned against the countertop, boots crossed, stuffing slices of pepperoni pizza with extra cheese into their mouths. And Chaz was seated on the bar top, heavy boots dangling. Pizza boxes lay open, and by the looks of it, they'd already been feasting.

"Do you want a plate?" Dylan asked Athena. "You don't have to eat like a caveman like my team."

"I'm good without one." She walked into the middle of the group and pulled out a slice of sausage and peppers. When she raised her gaze to his, her eyes twinkled. She took a bite.

After that, the ice was broken. Rocko struck up a conversation with her about Mardi Gras, which launched a conversation that had nothing to do with the mission or her boutique. Dylan was relieved by the guys' instincts.

He found an open spot on the counter to lean on. When Athena came to stand next to him, Ben arched a brow as if to say *I told you so.* Dylan shot him a warning glance.

They quickly emptied the pizza boxes, and Dylan lifted the last slice of sausage and pepper. He held it up to Athena. "You want it?"

She shook her head. "Two is plenty for me."

He skimmed his gaze over her figure. She could stand to gain a couple pounds, and if he had his way,

137

he'd have a whopping plate of shrimp and grits in front of her along with his *maman's* strawberry pie.

He looked up at a scuffling noise to see Rocko and Sean elbowing each other over the last slice.

"You had six slices, Rocko," Sean said.

"Pretty sure you did too," he drawled.

"I'm bigger, and I need the calories to keep going." Sean straightened his shoulders to prove it.

Ben grinned around the bite he'd just taken. "You guys are matched in size and strength. It's anybody's guess who'd win a fight."

"I'll bet ten dollars on Rocko." Chaz's words were met with a glare from Sean.

Roades slapped the countertop. "I'll float ten bucks on Sean."

"Guys, you can't throw down in the kitchen over a slice of pizza," Dylan said.

"We'll take it outside." Sean didn't look away from Rocko, whose grin hadn't wavered once.

"Remember that time you and Sean wrestled for an hour over the last donut?" Chaz tossed out to Dylan.

He slanted a look at Athena, who was watching the exchange with wide eyes. He said to her, "*Maman's* donuts are the *best*. They'd start a war, they're so good."

"They did start a war. Sean didn't speak to you for what—a month?" Ben asked.

138

"A week." Dylan's voice held a note of annoyance. Each time the story was recounted, the time period that his brother didn't talk to him bumped by a week.

"I think it was longer than that," Chaz said.

"Then there was that fight over that girl in Dylan's class. What was her name?" Ben looked around for someone to answer him.

"Haley," Rocko said.

Dylan gaped at him. "How the hell would you know? You didn't even grow up with us."

Rocko waved a hand. "I've heard it all."

"From who?" Dylan asked.

Blotches of red climbed his throat and spread over the stubble on his jaw until it reached his cheeks.

"Oh fuck." Dylan had that oh-shit feeling he always got when a guy was fucking with one of his sisters. He took a step toward Rocko. "Which sister is it?"

"What the hell? Sister?" Chaz hopped off the counter and faced Rocko. "You fucking with one of our sisters?"

"Can't be Tyler—she's safe in basic training," Sean interjected.

A groan sounded from Ben. "It better not be Lexi or you're gonna see the bad side of the Knights, buddy."

His warning hit Rocko, who threw up his hands. "Okay, guys, calm down. I only talk to your sisters at your family's gatherings. All innocent."

"Then why are you blushing?" Dylan demanded.

Rocko ran a hand over his face as if to erase the color. "Dude, nothing's going on. I swear. You know how both sisters get to talking and don't quit until you've heard every story in history."

Dylan looked to Ben, and they shared a nod. Yeah, the twins were definitely talkers. Even from the time they were little kids, they'd tell all the neighbors who visited their lemonade stand every word that had been exchanged in their house the previous day. That fact had even gotten their parents some phone calls from teachers at school.

"Okay, we'll buy that," Dylan said. He pointed at Rocko's chest. "But if we hear one word that you've been fucking around with either Tyler or Lexi, we'll each take a limb to break."

"I'm good at snapping femurs," Chaz added with a cheery tone that had Athena's head snapping to look at him.

"Chaz already claimed one of your femurs. Don't make us act on this threat, Rocko."

"Hell, you guys know how to ruin a man's appetite." Rocko pointed to the lone pizza slice. "It's yours, Sean."

Suddenly, Athena stepped up, grabbed the pizza and bit the point off it.

140

Everybody stared at her, jaws dropped. She smiled as she chewed. "There — I've ended the argument. Go back to being friends."

The chuckle started from Dylan and soon the guys were all laughing over the argument that had escalated to threats of bodily harm, even though the Knights were dead serious about Rocko staying away from their sisters. They'd had enough problems over the years that each brother took that shit seriously.

He wrapped an arm around Athena and drew her back to stand next to him. She continued to polish off the last piece of pizza, and Dylan noticed the room had grown quiet.

All the guys stared at them.

Damn, had he shown his feelings for Athena? Fact was, he wasn't sure he cared. Hell, he might already be too deep in her to climb out. If he had his way, he wasn't letting her go at all but in the event she decided otherwise, it would take him a long time to get over her.

She stood close, her shoulder against his arm for everybody to see.

Ben caught his eye. "Can I speak to the guys alone, Athena? Would you mind going into the other room?"

Dylan stiffened, and she stood straight. "Oh… sure." She glanced up at Dylan before heading into the living room.

Dylan leveled his stare at his oldest brother. "What crawled up your ass?"

Ben raised a brow, giving him a look he could only take seriously from a commander. Coming from a brother, Dylan would ignore anything he had to say.

"You can't fuck around with her, man," Ben said.

There was no point in denying he had taken her to bed and given her many delicious, screaming orgasms. "Whatever happens between Athena and me is none of your business."

Ben waved a hand. "It *is* my business—all of our business. Don't you see that if a threat walked into this room right now, you wouldn't stand here and fight with your team—you'd be running into the other room to protect your woman."

His woman. He liked the sound of that.

But Ben was wrong.

"You know Knight Ops comes first to me—always. Guts and glory, man."

"Guts and glory," Rocko echoed.

Dylan and Ben stared at each other a long minute. Finally, Dylan glanced at the rest of the group. "Anybody else feel the same way, speak up now."

Sean looked away and Chaz picked up an abandoned crust and stuffed it in his mouth. Roades and Rocko gave no indication of whose side they were on.

"If you're done accusing me of being a weak link in this team, then I'm going to check on Athena. I'm sure she overheard every word."

* * * * *

She had, and the pizza in her hand felt too heavy and cold. She set it on the end table, for lack of a better place to put it. She turned for her room, but Dylan stalked in, his gaze pinning her in place.

He moved to her, his jaw set. "It's none of their business."

"Dylan—"

He slammed his mouth over hers, shutting off any response. She gasped at the feel of his hard lips, and he slid his tongue into her mouth. Bending her over his arm, he kissed her like a man on a mission. Was he trying to prove something to her or to his team?

She pressed on his chest and he lifted his head. Eyes glazed, expression intense. "Dylan, your brother's right. We shouldn't—"

He kissed her again, drawing her onto tiptoe, swirling his tongue across hers until heat seeped low between her thighs and dampened her thong. She had no control over her arms when they wrapped around his neck and clung.

After several dizzying seconds, Dylan tore away from the kiss. "This isn't their business, Athena. It would be the same between us if we'd met at a dinner

143

party or in line for a ride on the Ferris wheel in Cajun Field." He flattened his palm to her spine and dragged her an inch closer until she knew nothing but his extreme body heat. "I want you, Athena, and that doesn't change a thing about this mission, and therefore is none of Knight Ops' business."

She didn't know how to respond to that, because her head and heart were racing. What was he telling her? She dared not let herself think too long about his words, yet...

"Speaking of the Ferris wheel. Do you have a coat? It's not storming right now, but it's good to be prepared."

"I— Where are we going?" She stared up at him, trying not to let her emotions get the best of her. Whatever was happening between her and Dylan might be real—or it might not. She needed to stay indifferent, and she was in limbo no matter what she did.

His eyes softened as he gazed down at her. "Get your coat, *cher.* We're going out."

Chapter Seven

Lights blurred past Athena's vision, and the scents of street foods filled her head. But all she could focus on was Dylan's hand in hers. Solid, warm. She was glad for the comfortable jeans, T-shirt and sneakers she'd thrown on after coming back to the safe house, because she planned to eat one of those caramel apples once they got off the Ferris wheel and would never have room in one of her fitted skirts.

She tugged on Dylan's hand, and he slowed, throwing a look over his shoulder. "I'm a little leery of heights."

"How leery?"

"Well," she looked up, up, up at the huge wheel lit with colored lights that seemed to soar into the sky, "I haven't been on one since I was fourteen, but I ended up practically sitting in my friend's lap."

"That's okay with me." He threw her a grin, and then concern drew his brows together. "If you don't want to go on the ride, we don't have to, *cher.*"

"Can we just walk around a bit first?" To get her gumption up. She didn't want to disappoint him since the idea had been his in the first place. And getting out of the safe house was exactly what she needed. After that argument between him and his brother, she was feeling punchy.

Dylan drew her through the crowd to a more open area. He kept glancing around, and she knew he was watching for threats.

"Nobody is going to find us in this crowd," she said.

His lips tipped slightly on one side. "Can't be too careful."

A few feet away, the orange of fire streaked through the darkening sky as three performers began to show off their skills, twirling flaming poles like batons and catching them. One exotic-looking female leaned backward and swallowed the flame. People cheered, and Athena found herself gripped with the excitement of Mardi Gras as she'd once experienced it as a little girl.

"My parents used to bring me every year," she said loud enough for Dylan to hear above the applause.

"Mine too. When we were old enough, they admitted they liked to stay away from the crowds and dropped off us boys with threats to behave."

She grinned. "And did you?"

"What do you think?"

She laughed. "I came with a few friends in my teen years, but we never got into trouble. The most I did was stare at people too long to see what they were wearing."

"So you were interested in fashion even then."

"Oh yes. I think it was my love of Mardi Gras that started my passion for all clothing you wear to celebrations. Weddings, parties and so much more."

He studied her for so long that she wondered if he thought she was crazy.

"I'm boring you."

He shook his head. "Not at all. I'm fascinated by you, Athena. Haven't you realized that yet?"

Before she could ingest those words or ponder what they meant, he towed her through the crush of people, past food vendors who showcased their frog legs or gator on a stick.

"You like gator?" he asked.

"Umm…"

"Forget about the ways you've eaten it before. When I take you to my family's cabin in the bayou, you can try my *maman's* and see that it really is good."

Again, she was shocked speechless. He was inviting her to his family's cabin and to share a meal with them? After the words that had passed between the Knights and Rocko, she was really curious about his sisters. Were they as strikingly good-looking as all the Knight brothers were? Her mind started pulling clothing options off her mental racks for the beautiful women.

They stopped to watch some young girls trying their hand at heaving a heavy mallet to win stuffed bears. When none of them succeeded, Dylan stepped up and threw down a bunch of bills.

"I'll have a couple tries."

Athena watched with amusement and awe as he won teddy bear after teddy bear and handed them out to the girls. When he finished, the game owner flexed his weak arms at Dylan and then gave him a thumb's up. The girls squealed and thanked him, and laughing, Athena and Dylan moved away.

After only an hour with him alone this way, away from the pressures of the safe house or all the surveillance and the intrigue that came with it, she was seeing a different side of Dylan.

And it was time to admit to herself she was falling for him. With or without the mess she was entangled in, she believed he was right to say that even if they'd met in line at the Ferris wheel, that things wouldn't be any different.

She tugged at his hand. "C'mon. Let's take that ride now."

He eyed her. "You're sure?"

"Yes."

Luckily, they didn't have to wait long to get on the ride, otherwise she might have chickened out. But once she was securely barred in next to Dylan with his arm firmly around her shoulders, she breathed in his scent and felt nothing but happiness. As they ascended, the city spread out before them, and she looked away from the shining lights and celebration below to stare into Dylan's eyes.

"Athena…" He caressed her lips with the rough pad of his thumb, shooting sparks through her system. His eyes glowed and not only with the reflection of the colored lights. Her heart beat faster as he leaned in to kiss her. His warm breath washed over her lips a second before they connected.

"*Cher,* I think I'm falling for you."

* * * * *

Dylan had been surrounded by the enemy in Afghanistan, been in the crosshairs of some asshole holed up in a bunker and experienced some near misses in Madrid when a mission went sideways. But right now, the hackles on his neck were standing straight up at full attention.

Fuck, he'd acted so far outside his training in bringing her here, and now he was going to pay for it. He'd have no choice but to let Ben in as well as Colonel Jackson. He could lose not only his post here protecting Athena but his place on the Knight Ops team.

But it was too late now. All he could do was take care of business while he was in the thick of it.

He shot a sideways glance at the man to his and Athena's left. The field was packed with people eating cotton candy and gasping at chainsaw jugglers.

So the chances of him seeing this guy twice now were slim.

Keeping a hand on Athena's back, he placed another on his weapon. Firing in a group of people like this was not an option, but he'd do what he had to if this guy made a move.

"I need to use the restroom," she said.

Fuck, now wasn't the time. He couldn't let her go into the building without cover. Somebody could be waiting in there for her. This guy in the plaid shirt with the sleeves ripped off wasn't doing a very good job of blending. Not when Dylan was trained to pick out anybody who looked suspicious. They were being followed, and he had to get her out of here.

"Okay, I'll wait right here." Not wanting to alert her to the danger quite yet, Dylan gave her a smile. She went into the restroom and he stood outside the door, trying not to eyeball the guy who was eyeing him.

Dylan casually pulled out his phone and dialed Ben.

"Yeah?" his brother answered.

"We're being followed."

"Fuck. Where are you?"

"The fair."

"Jesus, you're stupider when you're in love than I thought. Why would you risk taking her out of the safe house? You knew she was being watched."

In love? Dylan's mind tripped over his brother's words. Yes, he'd admitted he was falling, but he wasn't in that deep yet. Was he?

Fuck.

"I'm getting her out of here now and back to the safe house. I need an hour and then I'm going to Jackson."

"Jackson?" Ben echoed. "You're planning to get permission to end this, aren't you? You know what the colonel's going to say. You're fooling yourself if you think you can just take over the FBI's job on the investi—"

"I don't give a damn what it takes—I'm ending it. Give me an hour and a half and then pick me up at the safe house." Dylan ended the call, keeping his sights on the man in plaid from the corner of his eye. The man acted like he was intrigued by a group of kids arguing about which ride to go on next, but Dylan saw the hungry expression on his face. The asshole had found what he wanted.

Over Dylan's dead body would he let him take Athena.

She emerged from the restroom, and he slipped an arm around her. He could tell her what was going on, but that would only throw her into a whirlwind of fear. He wanted her not only calm but still experiencing the emotions they'd shared on the Ferris wheel. Because before Knight Ops showed up at the safe house to collect him, he wanted to take his leave of her properly... with passion and boundless pleasure.

His chest burned as he led her through the crowd. Judging by how she clutched his hand and brushed against him, she had no awareness of the situation or the thoughts running through his mind.

That she was so innocent, naïve and trusting almost killed him. The urge to surround her with big guys packing enough firepower to take out a small town was real.

"Are we leaving?" she asked as they passed the last concession stand.

He trailed a hand down her spine to the top of her buttocks, letting his touch speak for him. "I want to get you alone."

And safe.

And naked.

She arched a brow and threw him a secretive smile that would have his balls bluer than the Louisiana sky in the height of summer. But he couldn't think about his desires until he had her away from whoever was following them.

In the car, he took the craziest way home and quickly lost the guy on their tail. After a few minutes, he relaxed, able to breathe a bit easier knowing his skills were enough to continue keeping Athena safe.

Which brought him to other thoughts...

In love? Damn, Ben was an astute fucker. Even gripped by his feelings on the Ferris wheel, staring into Athena's dark eyes and tasting her sweet lips, Dylan hadn't realized the extent of his feelings. In one sentence his brother had left him with a perspective that only heightened his need to protect her.

Before they drove to the section of town where the safe house was located, he triple-checked that they weren't being followed. With the coast clear, he parked and took her inside. The locks on the door didn't seem like enough to keep her from harm.

She turned to face him, that tempting smile on her beautiful face.

He stepped forward, sliding a hand into her mass of hair and looking into her eyes. Yes, he had to end this at all costs. Even if whatever was between him and Athena ended after tonight, at least he'd walk away knowing she was safe.

* * * * *

Dylan stood before Athena, peeling her clothes off with his eyes. She wished he'd hurry up and do the job for real, because she was burning up.

She made a move for the hem of her top, but he caught her wrists. The small feeling of restraint sent a thrill through her, and her pussy squeezed. She dropped her head forward, afraid to speak and tell this man how bad she needed him. Since his confession on the Ferris wheel, she had thought of little else.

153

He hovered over her, nose brushing the fine hairs at her temple. "Don't move. Let me take off your clothes."

Her chest heaved with a breath she had to force past her lips. It was misery being so close to him and not being able to touch him let alone tear off both their clothes.

He took a step back, gaze roaming over her from head to toe as if deciding where to start. Finally, he moved forward again, drawing her tight against his body and claiming her mouth.

Each pass of his tongue across hers sent spikes of lust through her until she was out of her head. Gripping at his shoulders, a plea filled in her mind. She wanted his mouth all over her naked body and his cock buried deep in her pussy.

He nibbled at the corner of her lips and worked his way down her jaw to her throat. She angled her head to give him complete access. Gooseflesh broke over her, and it wasn't remotely chilly. In fact, it was the hottest night of the year so far and she could already hear the rumbles of thunder in the distance.

Running her hand up his spine, she held on to keep her knees from buckling as he reached a sensitive spot on her neck. A gasp left her, and he gave a rumble in answer.

"You taste so damn sweet." He licked down to her collarbone while working his hands under her top. She sucked in a sharp breath at the brush of callused fingers against her heated skin. Passion flooded her, and she dragged him closer.

"I need you, Dylan."

His hands stilled, his lips stopped working up and down the column of her throat.

"Please, I need you so bad."

"*Cher*... My God, I love to hear you beg." He lifted her, and she snapped her thighs around his hips as he carried her the few feet to the bed and laid her down. A wildness took hold of him, igniting her with the fever too. She dug her nails into his shoulders as he ripped away her clothes. When she lay bare for him, he parted her thighs.

Eyes glowing, he looked up at her. "I'm going to make you come twice at least on my tongue and then when I take you, you're going to be burning up for it."

"I already am."

His eyes sparkled with amusement. "We'll see about that."

When he dipped his tongue between her wet folds, she knew she was in for it because the man had thrown down a challenge and would never renege on his promise.

Crying out, she twisted the sheets in her fists. He slipped his tongue up and down with the slow passes that would drive a woman crazy. Her patience fled, and she thumped him with a fist on the shoulder.

"Dylan!"

"Mmm." He was in no hurry to get down to business. She wiggled and bucked her hips to bring his tongue into contact with the bundle of nerves that needed his touch so badly. Tingles raced through her, and her nipples throbbed.

As if knowing this, he reached up her body to strum each, back and forth as he finally opened his mouth over her clit and sucked it in.

Liquid heat enveloped her. She threw her head back as her pussy gave the first contraction. The rest hit with a force like the raging Louisiana storms, and she rocked her hips in time to each wave. He never released his suction on her clit and when he eased his fingers inside her, the second orgasm hit rapid-fire.

She writhed. He pressed his fingers downward on a spot that had her soaking wet in a blink. Breathless, she collapsed on the bed, only able to wiggle her fingers.

"That was two," she gasped.

He vibrated the inside her thigh with his chuckle, and pure happiness took over. She didn't have time now to absorb what was going on with her emotions, but the sensation deep in her heart wasn't something she'd ever felt before.

When he didn't move from between her thighs, she waggled her fingers at him again. "Dylan, don't make me wait another second!"

His chuckle turned into a full baritone laugh. Slowly, he moved to the side of the bed. How many times had she watched him strip off his clothes now? Each show seemed to get better, and she didn't know if she'd ever get enough of staring at that steely, tanned flesh.

At her place, she'd emptied her drawer of the condoms and laid several on the nightstand here in the safe house. He plucked one up with a crooked grin that melted her even more. Another look like that from him and she'd only be a puddle on the bed.

The veins in his forearms stood out as he stroked the condom down over his cock. Gripping the base, he moved over her.

"Arms above your head."

A shock went through her. "What?"

"Hold your arms over your head and don't move them until I tell you to."

Oh my God. She'd heard about guys taking control in the bedroom, but she'd never had the pleasure of finding one. Until now.

Locking gazes with him, she moved her arms upward. Heart thumping hard and fast, it took all her control not to yank him into her. The need to feel him stretching her doubled and then tripled.

"Dylan." Her voice came out as a reedy cry.

"*Mon Dieu*, I can't get enough of you." When he used his Cajun, she saw a bigger glimpse into the man's soul.

Bracing his weight over her, he poised his cock at her entrance. She spent several heartbeats lost in his

157

eyes, and just when she wasn't expecting it, he plunged into her.

She arched at the invasion, her pussy clutching at him as he immediately withdrew.

"I can't go slow. Fuck, I want to."

"Don't." She moved her arms to hold him, but he gave her a look that sent another spike of need through her.

"Don't move until I tell you." He sank back into her, hard and fast. Fucking faster with every stroke until she shook and rough growls erupted from his throat. She clung to the edge of another release, holding on to make it last.

He churned his hips, digging his cock so deep that she cried out.

"Hell. Athena, I can't hold back. Put your arms around me."

She did, and he lifted her off the bed, pounding furiously until her insides clenched hard on yet another orgasm. At that moment, he poured his release into her with untimed jerks of his hips. A low groan left him, and he went boneless atop her.

His weight was too much, and he rolled to the side, taking her with him. His eyes were still closed, the pulse pounding in his neck. For the first time, she realized he really was a man and not a machine—that he could actually be as tired as she was. Probably more.

She gave a deep sigh and entangled her legs with his.

He cracked an eye. "I hope that's a good sigh and not a disappointed one."

She grinned. "Did I sound disappointed to you?"

There it was—that grin. "No."

She stared at his hard lips that were incredibly soft when they needed to be. Leaning in, she kissed him softly. The tenderness she felt seeped into the caress. When she finally pulled away, he wrapped his hand around her nape and held her.

"I'm not done with you yet."

She hoped he wouldn't be done with her for a long time, but she was only fooling herself. This fling couldn't withstand the stress of the situation and bloom into more.

But as she relished his sweet kisses, all she could think about was how much she wished it could.

* * * * *

During this hell of the past few days, Dylan had been her only comfort, a rock in the sea that would toss her until she didn't know which direction to swim.

She shouldn't feel so broken but dammit, she did.

Pressing her fist to her lips, she tried for a few deep breaths of calm, but tears threatened. No, she couldn't be so upset by a stranger she didn't want to storm into her life in the first place finally walking out of it. It was just the emotions taxing her for a week finally reaching the surface. She—

"Hey. It's gonna be okay."

She jerked at the deep voice, so close to Dylan's. But she'd woken in the night to an empty bed and when she'd gone looking for him, she'd found Sean in his place. If not for the lamp burning in the living room, she might have mistaken his shape in the darkness for Dylan and embarrassed herself.

"Dylan had business to see to, but he'll be back."

"Does this have to do with how quickly we left the fair?"

"I'm not at liberty to disclose that information."

She hugged herself. After finding him gone, she'd armored herself in jeans, a T-shirt and a cardigan. Though the air was warm, the storms were back in full force, and her favorite natty sweater was the comfort Dylan couldn't offer.

She couldn't believe he'd left this way, without a word of goodbye. Was this how it would feel to be in love with a man like Dylan? Never knowing where he was or if he was doing something dangerous?

Of course he's doing something dangerous. It's his job.

Something tickled on her cheek and when she raised a hand to brush away a curl, she found tears drenching her skin. One dripped off her chin.

Sean moved closer. "May I?" He held out his arms, and she looked at that broad chest. She felt herself nodding and then he drew her head down on his chest and let her cry. "It's gonna be okay," he repeated soothingly.

"You sound like you do this all the time."

"No, just with my wife. She's full of pregnancy hormones right now. Oh. I shouldn't have let that slip. Nobody knows it yet, so just don't tell my brothers, all right?"

She nodded against his chest. "I didn't know you were married." Actually, she didn't know anything about Dylan's family—or him outside of this mess she was tangled in. Who was he really?

"We've been married two months now. We found out about the baby the same week, and I'll tell you, that hit me hard. In this line of work, until you have something to lose, you don't know how every second counts. Now I have more reasons to keep from being reckless."

"Do you think all your brothers feel that way? That they have a lot to lose and have to be careful?" He smelled like clean cotton and she was glad for the brotherly comfort because she was afraid of his answer. If she learned Dylan took risks... She swallowed hard.

"I'm sure Ben does. And if I'm not wrong, Dylan does too."

She drew back. "What does that mean?"

He smiled softly, his lips a bit thinner and harder looking than Dylan's. Then again, she'd believed the man she'd kissed—oh, so many times—to be carved

161

from granite. That meant Sean was flesh and blood as well.

"Don't you know why you're so broken up that Dylan left? Or why he looked about to put a fist through a cement block wall?" His hazel eyes gleamed with a kindness that made her tears flow faster.

She shook her head. "He looked like that?"

"I don't think I'm wrong in saying you've been more to my brother since he met you."

Talking to a stranger this way—and a male too—was disconcerting, so why did she feel her mouth opening and words tumbling out?

"There's an attraction, yes. But it's not real. It's from the stress and being thrown together for so many days."

He stared at her. "Are you sure that's all? Sometimes things happen fast, especially if they're meant to be."

She drew away. "I don't know anything anymore. I've had so many days cooped up here that I can't think straight. Especially when he touches me..." She trailed off and looked up at Sean, embarrassed. "You don't need to know the details. I'm sorry."

His warm smile was back, coupled with a crease between his brows. "It's all right. I guessed anyway."

"Does the whole Knight Ops team know?"

He lifted a shoulder in a shrug. "They do if they've been paying attention."

"What does that mean? Are we that obvious?" She almost changed her words to *were we that obvious* because she and Dylan were over. She couldn't deal with a man leaving in the middle of the night and not telling her where he was going or if he'd ever return.

She swiped another tear away as it dribbled down her cheek.

Sean rubbed her shoulders, his strong hands finding all the knots she didn't know she had. A sigh left her.

"Look, we're brothers. Even Rocko might as well be blood. We know each other inside and out and you see changes in people."

"You saw changes in Dylan?"

He nodded. "He's been different. He's always been the quietest Knight. God knows our sisters are anything but quiet. But he's been even quieter when he's around us. He's also moodier."

She tensed. "I make him moodier?"

Sean grinned, the smile line cutting through his cheek so much like Dylan's that her heart flipped over. "Don't you know love makes a man moodier?"

She blinked.

"You didn't know how he feels?"

"I—" She looked up at him, unable to find the words with the big L word flashing in her head like a neon sign on a carnie booth.

She drew a deep breath to control the crazy notions circling her head. This was Sean speaking and not Dylan. He didn't really know how his brother felt unless Dylan confided, and it sounded as if that wasn't the case.

He must be misinterpreting his brother's silence and moodiness. Heck, he hadn't even been around him that much lately. How could this be love when she and Dylan had just met and were in a situation that was a breeding ground for emotional turmoil?

Then again...

She pushed out a breath. "He told me he's falling for me."

He grunted. "That's what I thought at first too with Elise. I thought it couldn't be anything but lust and a heavy crush. Damn, was I wrong. But it didn't take me long to figure things out, and since Dylan and I share DNA, I bet he's the same way."

Athena shook her head. "Nothing can happen between us."

He cocked his head, watching her closely. "Why not? Are you attached?"

"No! I mean, of course not. I wouldn't play around with Dylan if I was. But... it isn't real. These feelings." A cry bubbled up her throat, and she narrowly cut it off before breaking down entirely. She rubbed a hand over her face. "Look, I'm exhausted. I should get some sleep and I'm thinking about closing the boutique tomorrow."

He pressed his lips together. "I'm sorry, but you can't do that."

"I can't?" She gaped at him. She could set her own hours. Never once had she chosen not to open Athena's Creations or left early in all her years until this week.

"Athena, we're trying to find the people who are not only on our watch list but our targets. When they send in Knight Ops, we have a duty to smoke out the criminals and capture them. In this case, your customers."

Once again, her guard went up. Her clients weren't criminals, just people who loved to flaunt their money.

She shook her head.

He nodded. "There are things we can't tell you."

"Dylan mentioned that." A pang hit her at saying his name.

"We need you to keep your normal business hours and stick to the plan with us. Did Dylan mention he also needs you to place another order to that supplier you purchased the jeweled shoes from?"

She shook her head, exhausted and drained. How was she going to make it through the next day feeling this way? And without Dylan to push her.

Sean squeezed her shoulder. "I have a plan."

She met his stare.

"I'm bringing in backup, someone to help you in the boutique."

Her brows shot up.

165

He grinned. "My wife. She's OFFSUS too."

"OFFSUS. I keep hearing that word but I don't know what it means and nobody will tell me." She folded her arms over her chest again, trying to find comfort in the natty sweater. But only having Dylan close right now would drive away this panic rising inside her.

"I shouldn't be telling you this. It stands for Operation Freedom Flag Southern US."

"So you're like... Homeland Security?"

The crooked smile he wore was so like Dylan's that she had to squeeze herself harder to keep from running to the door and out of the house to look for him.

"You could say we're an amped up version of that crew."

"How amped up?" She thought of Dylan's muscles as he thrust into her.

"Think of it this way—they're mall cops and we're Knight Ops."

* * * * *

Ben, Chaz and Roades stared at Dylan while Rocko just leaned against the wall, a grin plastered on his face. For ten minutes they'd been trying to talk him out of confronting Colonel Jackson, but they were wasting their breath. They were told Jackson was en route to the base, and Dylan was climbing the walls waiting.

166

"Think about it, Dylan," Ben said for the third time.

"I have thought about it. This is dragging on. If we'd held back and waited on that mission overseas—"

Ben sliced a hand through the air to cut him off. "That's completely different and you know it."

"The threat isn't small or we wouldn't be here discussing it right now. Jackson felt it was important enough to set us on the path and we've been running in place for days. I'm fucking done churning up dirt."

"Dammit, you know what you did was wrong. Taking her out of the safe house to a fucking public place? And Mardi Gras, the biggest security threat in the country—hell, maybe even the planet? This isn't going to go unanswered for."

"I'll deal with the fallout if it comes to that."

"Oh it will. You're not thinking straight because you're in—"

"If it isn't the Knight Ops boys. To what do I owe the pleasure of this visit?" Jackson's voice cut off what Ben was about to say, but Dylan could guess. They'd spent the past ten minutes trying to convince him that his emotions were making him act irrationally. But from Dylan's point of view, he was the only clear-thinking one of the bunch. Lying in wait was not their style and never would be. Why were they stalling now?

Jackson waved them into his office and circled to his desk. The team gathered around, shoulder to shoulder, at attention.

"At ease, men. Now somebody explain what the hell you're doing in my office."

The colonel didn't hold back even though the captain of the Knight Ops team was his own son-in-law. In fact, he was probably harder on Ben because of it.

Jackson looked from face to face. "Well? Dylan, shouldn't you be at the safe house?"

"I left Sean in charge, sir."

"I was awakened in the middle of the night after receiving a phone call from Ben." He directed his stare at their caption. "That you had disobeyed direct orders and taken the woman you're charged with out of the safe house and to the fucking fair?"

"Sir, I—" Dylan began, heat infusing his face. He'd done it, all right. Fucked up bad. He had no excuses other than he wanted to see her happy, and he'd achieved that at least.

"You what? Screwed up? I'd say that's an understatement, Knight."

"It won't happen again, sir. I will take whatever punishment is coming to me."

Jackson eyed him for a long minute. "Damn right you will. I should take you off the operation."

"Sir, that isn't necessary. I'll scrub latrines, whatever it takes."

168

He shook his head. "Goddamn latrines," he muttered.

"Sir, I request that you do not remove me from the operation. What I did was wrong. I acted irresponsibly and beyond my authority."

"I'll deal with that later. Right after you tell me why you dragged me out of bed to come down here."

Dylan shot Ben a look and received a warning glance in return. But he stepped up to the desk and took charge. "Sir, I'm asking permission to act fast. The vendor of those jeweled shoes and some of the other necklaces in Athena's Creations has a false front."

"I knew that from the report, Knight." If Jackson had been pulled from his bed to come to the base and have this conversation, he didn't look it. He was just as sharp and eagle-eyed as ever.

"Why haven't we reacted to that intel? The address leads to a warehouse."

"The warehouse was already inspected. It checked out as being a storage facility for a local department store."

He shook his head. "I don't buy that, sir. With all respect to the investigators—"

"Are you saying our people are wrong, Knight?"

He held his breath. Then let it go.

"That's what I'm saying, sir. Requesting permission to search the warehouse."

"Denied. Now I'm going back home and get into bed. There's still," he checked his gold watch, "three hours left before dawn. Now get out of my office, men."

The guys filed out, and when Dylan didn't budge from the spot, Ben grasped his shoulder, each fingertip bruising. He knew when he removed his shirt, he'd be wearing four blue crescent marks.

Dylan turned for the door and didn't stop walking until they were outside.

Ben glared at him. "That went well."

He ran his fingers over his hair. "If this was Dahlia, you wouldn't be standing there saying this to me. You'd have the hammer back as you ran into that warehouse."

"So you're admitting your feelings for the woman?" Ben asked.

"Look, are we new recruits on the bus about to be greeted by the drill instructor? Or are we fucking Knight Ops?"

Rocko was nodding. "I'm with ya, Dylan."

Chaz hesitated only a heartbeat before stepping up. "Me too."

"Goddammit, you fuckers are going to get us court martialed," Ben rumbled.

Roades shook his shoulders as if limbering up for the fight. "Then we go down swingin'. Let's go, Ben."

Dylan yanked open the door of the black SUV and climbed behind the wheel. Chaz tried for shotgun, but Ben leveled a look at him that sent him to the back seat.

"I'm still the fucking captain of this team even if there's a fucking mutiny at the moment. You'd better be fucking right about this, Dylan."

He started the engine. "How many times you going to say fuck in the same paragraph? *Maman* would wash your mouth out with soap."

"She's too busy washing out Lexi's. Since Tyler's in Boot Camp, she's decided she needs to step up and fill her sister's shoes," Chaz added.

"Jesus, is that right?" Dylan asked.

"Yes." The answer came from Rocko, which earned a collective growl from the brothers.

"Didn't we tell you to stay away from our little sister?" Ben twisted in the seat to glare at their team member.

Dylan glanced into the rearview mirror to see Rocko kicked back, relaxed. When he didn't answer, Dylan's brothers started arguing the point. But Dylan just focused on the road and drove. His mind was back with Athena. Sean would keep her safe—he had no worries on that front.

He wasn't wrong in paying a visit to the warehouse, permission or not. He had to end this. Breaking some faces would feel pretty damn good right about now too.

The argument continued until the time he rolled up a block from the building. He cut the engine and turned in his seat to look at the men.

"Roades, you cut the security cameras."

"Done." He saluted Dylan.

"Chaz, you're with Ben, Rock with me. Roades, as soon as you get those wires cut, we rally and go in together."

"What are we looking for?" Chaz asked.

"Anything the investigators would have missed."

"Wait a damn minute here. I'm still in charge of this team." Ben's voice stopped the conversation.

"Fine, then you're responsible for getting us in and getting what we need," Dylan said.

"All right."

They all waited for his command.

Ben rubbed his knuckles over his jaw. "I'm not exactly sure what to look for either."

Dylan gave a shake of his head. He'd say *I told you so* later, after Ben had a couple beers in him to soften the blow.

He looked at his team. "Look for labels that seem out of place or boxes with no labels at all. I think what we're looking for would be hidden among the other crates."

"And if we run into anybody?" Roades asked.

"Then we secure the threat." Dylan's no-nonsense tone was answered with no-bullshit nods. He put his hand on the door handle. "Let's roll."

Entering was a breeze and they shined flashlights on crate after crate, searching for something out of the ordinary. Roades took down one box and sliced it open, pulling out a plastic bag of men's socks.

"This what we're looking for, Dylan?"

"No, dickhead, it's not and you know it. Stay on task." Dylan moved through the towers of crates, reading labels. Suddenly, a sound made him stop dead. He jerked his head to the side.

"Keep low, weapons at the ready." Ben's quiet command came to them.

A box teetered and fell, making a loud thump on the concrete floor. Two guys rushed out from one aisle and then Knight Ops was in the thick of it.

Dylan pulled up and took aim. He ignored the throbbing of his heart and slowed his breathing for a split second before he took the shot. The man fell on his side and didn't move again.

"Nice shot." Rocko flashed a grin before sprinting after an assailant.

Dylan assessed the situation in a blink, tracking his own men and zeroing in on the enemy. Apparently these guys didn't approve of somebody scoping out their warehouse and were armed for a damn good reason.

Because they had something to hide.

173

The faintest sound of a boot scuffing against concrete had him spinning. He whipped around his rifle and smashed the butt over the man's eye. He screamed as bone shattered and dropped to his knees.

"I've got a prisoner," Dylan called to his team.

"Good. Get him talkin'," Ben responded.

On high alert for other attackers, he kicked the guy in the shin. "On your feet."

When he didn't move, Dylan commanded, "Now or I'll find someone else to let live long enough to tell me what I need to know."

The man swayed to his feet, blood dripping down his face from the butt to the face.

"Show me where the goods are."

"You can't steal them."

Ah, so they believed they were being robbed. They were just a bunch of bodies standing guard.

Using this to his advantage, he shoved the man forward. "Take me to the goods."

To his right, another shot exploded, and he jerked his head around. Roades had a guy pinned down around a huge crate. If the guy got desperate as a last chance at survival, things would get ugly.

Dylan had to do something. "I've got a clear shot."

Roades' voice came back gritty with suppressed fury. "Take it."

He got the guy in his sights and took him out with a hit to the right shoulder, through the meaty part where no vitals were. Roades rushed around the corner and jumped the guy, confiscating his weapons and using zip-ties to immobilize him.

Dylan nudged his captive. "Get goin'."

With a hand still holding his pulverized eye, he moved forward. They walked the length of one row of crates to the end and then turned right. Up another aisle.

"If you're trying to throw me off, don't bother. You can't."

"Just let me leave with my life. We're supposed to guard this stuff but it isn't worth never seeing my wife again."

Dylan had a moment of remorse for hitting the guy, yet this was a battle and he couldn't stop to think about anything but the mission and Knight Ops.

"Just show me and things won't get out of hand."

"Come out, you fucking cowards!" someone screamed, and it wasn't any of the Knights or Rocko.

A shot went wild, followed by two more blasts. Dylan heard the telltale *whoosh* of bullet cutting through flesh. Then a thump as a body fell.

The man in front of him pointed at a box.

"Get it down," Dylan ordered.

The man took his hand away long enough to reach up for a box wedged between two. Nothing out of the ordinary here, no markings to indicate it was anything but more socks.

Dylan took it from him, prepared for more physical blows. But the man just stood waiting for him to flip open the lid.

Revealing more gems.

"You're laundering these. Why? And for who?" Dylan's demands had the man shaking his head.

"I don't know, man. I only guard the stuff."

"You don't even know who signs your paychecks?"

He shook his head. "We get paid in envelopes left in a locked box in the office." He held his eye again, grimacing. It had to hurt like hell.

"There are more of these. Show me where they all are."

He nodded and half an hour later, the team had every hostile guard subdued and a virtual pirates chest of treasure spread out on a metal table.

"Jesus." Ben blew out a whistle. "Gotta be millions worth here."

"Yeah, but why? Think our intel's still correct? Who is funding this operation and is the money only going as an investment to gain more? Shut down that power grid and all the banks and then wipe them out?"

Ben shook his head. "Above our pay grade. I'm sure you could find out with enough time to hack some systems, though."

Dylan grunted.

"Let's pack these up and get them to Jackson. I have a feeling there are more microchips inside some of the gems. The intelligence officers will have their work cut out for them." Ben twitched two fingers toward the exit, indicating they should move out.

He was right that Dylan could uncover more about this, but what he most wanted to know was which of Athena's customers was really moving the jewels. The woman who'd acquisitioned the shoes had gone underground it seemed, vanished off the face of the earth. He had a feeling there was more than one customer using Athena's Creations as a way to move funds, and he just had to keep Athena out of it... safe.

Chapter Eight

"Athena, meet Elise. She's got certain skills that will help us to root out the people we're looking for. Besides that, she happens to be the mother of my unborn child and has some mean jujitsu skills." Sean beamed at his wife.

From his words, Athena should find Elise to be intimidating, but the woman smiled at her, dissipating the nervousness of meeting someone new.

Athena extended a hand and Elise shook it. "It's nice to meet you."

"Sean's filled me in on what's happening here. I'm happy to help with whatever you need me to do."

Athena cleared her throat and turned to Sean. "Thank you, but... what do you mean that Elise has certain skills to help root out the people you're looking for?"

"She could interrogate the shell off a snail, and she will be talking to your customers."

This couldn't end well. Either she'd piss off a bunch of clients who'd never walk through her door again or she'd end up with calls from their lawyers. When wealthy people got pissed, they got their lawyers involved.

"I don't think this is such a good idea," she started.

Elise placed a warm hand on her arm and gave her a warmer smile. "I promise they won't know what hit them. I have my ways, Athena. If you'll trust me, I believe I can speed along this process so you get your life back faster."

Oh God, she'd said the magic words. All Athena wanted was for things to return to normal.

But that would mean Dylan was no longer in her life.

She couldn't live in this limbo anymore more. The only answer was to agree.

She nodded, and Elise patted her arm. "Let's get started then. Sean?" She nodded toward the office, and he faded away behind the scenes. Elise smoothed a hand over her slim-fitting dress. She didn't look pregnant, only slender and glowing.

"First, do I look like I'd be your employee?" she asked.

Athena nodded. "Yes, you play the part well."

"Good. I admit I know nothing of clothing designers or what you might use in your own creations. So I'll leave the clothes up to you and I'll do the talking."

"All right." Athena felt strangely energized being around this woman. Maybe she'd been running a business on her own too long or the stress of being around all males twenty-four-seven had finally worn her down. Either way, she was excited to see what Elise would do today.

Three hours later, the customers were buying more, adding on whole outfits that Athena suggested while Elise talked their ears off about their families, jobs and even political affiliations. All done in her suave way.

After Athena rang out another big order, she flashed Elise a grin. The customer left, and she leaned against the counter, satisfied. "We make a great team. Sure you don't want to quit your day job?" she asked Elise.

The woman laughed with a toss of her head. "It's more like a night job most of the time. I'm still not sure how we're handling a baby."

She eyed her. "You didn't plan to start a family then?"

Elise laughed again. "I sure hope you're ready to be carrying Dylan's child."

Her eyes bulged. "What?"

"You're sleeping with him, aren't you? Not that I can say anything—these Knight boys have something you just can't ignore."

A flush stole over Athena's throat and face. "Yes, but... we use birth control."

She barked another laugh. "Honey, so was I. I had implants, for God's sake, and still Sean's sperm made it through. After I threw up once, I went directly to the doctor and he confirmed the pregnancy and removed the implants. No harm done to the fetus since we caught it so early."

Athena's brows shot up. "You got pregnant on heavy birth control?"

"I'm telling ya, the Knight gene pool is strong."

Athena's stomach flipped over at the thought of carrying Dylan's child. Of being bound to the man she wanted on such a raw, basic level that it blasted her every time she thought about it.

Elise tipped her head as she examined Athena. "I never thought of Dylan choosing a woman like you, but I see it now."

She blinked. "What do you see?"

"You're gorgeous in such an exotic way, and he's got a deep case of wanderlust. Settling with you would feel like he's always wandering a new place, exploring."

She gulped.

"But you're smart too, Athena. And he'd be deeply attracted to your brain. Dylan is unmatched for intelligence among the Knights."

Suddenly, Elise jerked a hand up to her ear. She flashed a grin at Athena and whispered, "My husband opposes what I just said. Let me try again— all the Knights' intelligence surpasses their good looks."

She slapped her hand over her ear again, and Athena realized she must be wearing an earpiece that

Sean was speaking into. Elise gave a low chuckle but didn't speak to her husband again.

The conversation between her and Athena ended too when Mrs. Landrenau entered the boutique. As soon as Athena greeted her, she realized Elise was watching them too closely. Did she suspect this kind woman as being one of the players in the terrorist activity? Impossible. Athena had known the Landrenaus for years.

"Athena, how lovely you look today." Mrs. Landrenau beamed at her.

Athena thought she must need an eye examination, because the night had taken its toll on her. Hell, the week had taken its toll on her.

"Thank you. What brings you into the store again?"

Elise stepped in then, and Athena didn't need to ask why. Elise suspected her.

Now that Athena considered it, maybe the woman *had* frequented her shop more than usual lately.

Athena slanted a glance at Elise. "Uh, you haven't met my new employee yet. Ann Marie, this is Mrs. Landrenau."

Elise didn't miss a beat at Athena's newly concocted name for her. She smiled widely and took Mrs. Landrenau's hand. As Elise struck up a conversation, she couldn't help but think of Sean in the office, taking note of every single word exchanged.

Athena broke in, "Mrs. Landrenau, it's fantastic to see you, but I didn't expect you today. Did you get invited to a last-minute party and need a dress?"

The banker's wife smiled and sailed through the room in her elegant way. "I was hoping you would have some shoes for me to go with a dress I got elsewhere. This is the dress." She leaned in to share a photo on her phone.

Athena nodded. "I'm sure we can find something that will set off that beautiful gown."

"Something with rhinestones or jewels?"

Elise's head snapped up. This is it, her eyes seemed to say. She twitched her head to the side, and Athena knew Sean was speaking into her ear.

Athena had to play it cool and help in any way she could. She waved at Mrs. Landrenau, but Elise jumped in.

"Why don't I show you some of our new shipment of high heels? You'll never believe how gorgeous these jewels are!" Elise led her to the shoe wall.

After only a few steps, the woman straightened and looked around herself as though confused. "Oh dear, I just remembered I have an appointment in ten minutes and I'm going to be late. I don't know how it slipped my mind…"

Oh God, was the banker's wife the one who Knight Ops was looking for? And her husband too? Mrs. Landrenau strode to the exit.

Athena bustled after her, wondering if she should try to restrain her from leaving.

Elise caught Athena's eye, though, and she didn't want to see Elise's jujitsu skills today. So Athena said a feeble farewell to the woman as she practically ran out of the boutique.

Elise leveled her gaze on Athena. "That's our woman."

Athena opened her mouth to speak, but no words came out.

"Sean says we need to abort and get you to safety."

All the blood drained from Athena, and she swayed as a thought hit her. "Oh my God."

Elise clutched her arm, holding her steady. "What is it? Did you think of something?"

"She asked about jeweled shoes and Knight Ops confiscated that pair. Sean said they're connected to the terrorist activity in some way, though he hasn't completely explained how. But the vendor who sold me those also had some necklaces."

"Here in the store?" Elise started moving toward the jewelry case, but Athena grabbed her arm.

"No, they took those too. But there's one they missed."

Elise stared at her.

"In my apartment."

"Fuck. I have to get you there and get the necklace now. Sean, do you hear me?"

He appeared at their sides, looking as dark and dangerous as Athena had seen Dylan look that day when he'd ripped open the closet door and found her hiding there.

"There's a necklace at your apartment?" he asked.

She nodded. "I took it home to match fabrics to it. I was going to make it into a choker neckline of a gown, but I forgot I had it. With Mardi Gras being my busy time and..." She trailed off as the special ops people around her broke into action.

Elise grabbed her by the arm and started towing her to the back door while Sean jogged to the front and locked up. In seconds, Athena was in the back seat of a car whooshing over the rain-covered streets of New Orleans headed toward her apartment.

"Give me Ben," Sean demanded into his cell. He quickly filled Ben in and then held the phone away from his ear. He shot a look at Elise in the passenger's seat. How the woman looked so cool and composed, Athena couldn't guess. She felt like a nervous wreck. Even her hair seemed to be reacting by standing out in a frizzy mass from the humidity in the air.

"What's going on?" Athena leaned forward between the front seats.

Sean sliced a look her way. "Dylan's going nuts knowing you're in the wind and can't protect you. He's coming."

* * * * *

"Put it on speaker." Dylan's command came out as a bark, and Ben didn't even give him shit about taking over as he pushed a button on the phone.

Elise's voice filled the SUV.

"You get the necklace, Athena. Sean, you got the door."

The trio was inside Athena's apartment, and Dylan could picture it clearly as he listened. His shoulder muscles screamed with tension, and he had taken a hell of a blow to the ear that had rung his bell back in that warehouse. His eardrum was still humming, but he focused on Elise's voice.

"It's all right," he heard her say to Athena. "Calm down, honey. Your hands are shaking so bad you'll never be able to open that drawer if you don't take some deep breaths."

"Goddammit," Dylan bit off. He needed to be there with her. Holding her. Keeping her safe.

Ben threw him a *hold onto your feelings* look.

"Athena, what are we looking for? A case?"

"No..." The sound of Athena's voice slammed Dylan. His chest burned with the need to release a battle cry and get to her faster.

186

"In this drawer? Let me open it—you're shaking so bad."

Dylan gripped the steering wheel so hard it felt like it might snap under his hands. He hoped it would—he needed to hit, shoot, destroy. The fight back in that warehouse hadn't touched the adrenaline boiling in his system.

"She's reaching into the drawer," Elise told them. "She's got a book. Wait—are you fucking kidding me?"

Stunned silence swelled on Elise's end.

"Holy hell," she whispered.

"Tell us what is going on," Dylan demanded.

"She's got a necklace worth half a million dollars stuffed into the crack of a novel."

"And a two worthless wedding bands in her safe. Jesus." Dylan winced as he rubbed his jaw, which was also bruised.

"Let me see it," Elise said to Athena. A second of pause. And then, "Athena, we need a hammer. Do you have one? Hurry."

Ben and Dylan exchanged a look. What the hell did they need a hammer for? He imagined all kinds of threats pouring through the door of her apartment, Sean's ass kicked and him lying on the floor, leaving Elise and Athena alone. Elise was bad-ass, but that didn't mean Dylan was comfortable with her as Athena's sole protector.

187

He slammed the heel of his hand onto the steering wheel and Ben uttered, "Stop. Wait for it."

"Okay, good. That's a good hammer. Now I want you to smash the third gem. Right here."

"What the fuck?" Dylan exploded.

"Smash it?" Athena's stunned tone filled him with longing.

"Do it," Elise ordered.

A loud crack sounded.

"Oh my God, what is that?" Athena asked.

Dylan stomped the gas pedal, speeding through the streets faster than ever.

"It's a microchip. Sean, we need to get out of here. Now."

"Bingo," Chaz said from the back of the SUV. "Your girlfriend found it, Dylan."

His mind barreled forward. "Tell her to call the customer back and say you've got a necklace for her to see, that you just got it in. Then string what's left of it back together. We'll meet you at the boutique."

"We're walking out now." A minute later, Elise had placed the phone on speaker as well, and she and Sean were arguing about the fastest route to take.

"Athena, are you okay?" Dylan asked.

"Y-yes."

His heart lodged in his throat.

"They knew she had it," Sean said.

"So why didn't they toss her apartment?" asked Roades.

"Because she's just the middle man. They knew she'd keep it safe until the time they needed it, and then they sent the Landrenau woman to retrieve it today." Ben said everything that Dylan had been thinking.

Dylan snorted. "The damn woman keeps junk store rings in her safe and an expensive necklace worth way more than the gems stuffed in a book."

"I thought it was costume jewelry, Dylan! Not everybody is as cynical about the world as you!"

A laugh burst from him, relief taking hold as her sassy retort filled the SUV. It also aroused the hell out of him. The minute he resolved this and got her alone...

"Athena, call the customer and tell her to bring her hubby to the boutique. Say there's a necklace you want her to see and also a matching tie pin."

"Brilliant, *cher*," Sean told his wife.

"Give me that phone," Athena demanded.

Dylan found his voice around the swelling of pride in his chest. His little boutique owner was turning out to be one hell of a spy. "Guts and glory, guys. We'll see you there."

* * * * *

Athena didn't think her fingers could get any icier. She turned to Elise. "I don't think I can do this. How do I face her? I'm not a good actor."

Elise placed her hands on Athena's arms. "You're doing fantastic, better than we expected. In fact, maybe we'll make it a family operation soon and bring you in."

She started shaking her head to dispute Elise's words, not totally wrapping her head around any of it.

"Just a bit longer. You only need to show the Landrenaus the jewels." They'd fished out a tie pin with a bright ruby that was not from the same fake vendor but a legitimate jeweler.

"I—" All the air rushed from Athena as she looked up into a set of deep hazel eyes. "Dylan," she breathed.

Elise stepped aside just in time, because the man would have bowled her over.

Dylan stormed across the boutique and caught Athena up in his strong arms. The breath whooshed from her as her breasts were flattened against his hard chest and his masculine scent enveloped her.

She gazed up at him, shock stealing over her mind like a white fog. "You're bleeding."

He cupped her face and slammed his mouth over hers. Tingles of electricity shot from his mouth to her nipples and straight to her pussy. She gasped, and he thrust his tongue into her mouth. She was vaguely aware of a male chuckle coming from one of his brothers as she wrapped her arms around him and held on tight.

The kiss was full of apology and sweetness and the promise of what Dylan could do to her in the hot, sticky Louisiana night to come.

"Dude, you'd better break it off." The order cut through the sexual haze they shared, and Dylan released her.

He stepped back, gaze burning into her.

"Yeah." His voice was gritty. "That's how it's gonna be as soon as we're alone. Now come with me."

He took her by the arm and strode quickly through the showroom into the office. He whipped open the closet.

"What? I'm supposed to lure the Landrenaus—"

He gave a shake of his head. "You're going to stay safe."

"I can do this, Dylan," she began.

He firmed his jaw. "I can't have you out in the open when shit goes down. Now get in the closet and I'll come get you when it's done." He gave her a nudge toward the opening. At the office door, he turned. "And don't worry about anybody getting in here. They'll have to go through me."

Shaky again from Dylan's kisses and the fear of what was about to happen, she ducked into the closet, sank to a crouch and closed the door. What a turn of events, with her back where she'd started again. Now she was so much smarter about what went on in the world, and while the universe didn't have the same rainbow-colored filter it once had in her eyes, she held hope.

Hope for a future with Dylan.

* * * * *

"Get behind that counter, Elise, and don't move unless I tell you to." Sean's order had all of the Knight Ops team looking at him.

"She's pregnant," Sean announced. "I won't have her in jeopardy."

"Holy hell. Congrats, guys. We didn't know," Ben said.

Sean flashed a brief smile. "We haven't told *Maman* or *Pére* yet, so don't say anything."

Chaz had his sights trained on the front door of the boutique. "I'm a little busy right now. They're coming."

Heart thundering, Dylan waited. When the door opened, the back door burst open at the same time.

Dylan didn't have any choice—he had to fight with his team. Athena would be safe long enough for him to kick some ass and get back to her.

"Roades, Rocko!" he shouted, weapon trained on the opening as he ran for the back room. His team flanked him. Thugs flooded the space.

"You're outnumbered," Dylan called out. "Surrender and nobody gets hurt!"

Of course there was that one stupid fucker with no common sense. He squeezed off a shot, and Dylan took him down with a bullet to the knee. His leg collapsed as his bone and joint shattered, and he screamed.

From the front of the building, another shot exploded, and Dylan's heart seized up.

He'd walked away from the door of the office. Somebody could be finding Athena's hiding spot right now.

"You got this?" he shouted to Roades.

Roades threw him a grin and whipped out some zip-ties. "Get on your knees, hands behind your backs, boys."

Dylan ran out and into the thick of a shootout. Ben and Sean had taken cover behind counters, and one glass case was completely shattered, glass glittering like diamonds on the floor.

He ran to the office and peeked in. Relief hit as he realized nobody had breached this spot yet. If someone had, he'd kick himself for this error for the rest of his life.

And he'd spend the entirety making it up to Athena too. First, with a ring and then the most beautiful, safest home he could provide. With three— no four—German Shepherds.

After that, they'd get busy on those babies. His *Maman* would be happy to hear that the family tree was branching out.

He focused on Landrenau. The man was decked out in a fine suit he'd probably dropped a grand on at least right here in this shop. On the surface, he looked like a man with swagger, but his eyes burned with hate as he wielded an automatic weapon.

"Get us the necklace and that tie pin and nobody gets killed."

They still thought the tie pin was a real item they needed.

Chaz zipped across the room, as silent and stealthy as a panther stalking prey. The Landrenaus and the three men with them didn't even notice him. If Dylan hadn't been looking, he wouldn't have noticed either.

He slashed a look toward where Chaz had disappeared. Knight Ops had been pinned down in much worse situations, but he still couldn't risk a single bullet piercing their hides, and therefore he had to wrap up this threat.

He stepped forward and lowered his weapon. "We'll give you the necklace and pin."

Ben looked at him as if he'd lost his mind.

Ignoring him, Dylan said, "We know these items are worth way more money than they look. There was a microchip embedded in one of the jewels of the necklace as well as the shoes."

194

The banker's face drained of color. "Where are they?"

"They're being analyzed." Dylan casually walked to the front counter where Athena had been standing when he arrived and he assumed the items were.

"So even if I give you these," he held up the two sparkling accessories, "we will find you. And hunt you down. And you will spend the rest of your lives in prison, where you won't have the expensive things you're used to. But if you choose to back down now and come with us, there's a plea bargain in your futures."

Husband and wife exchanged looks.

"Make your call," Dylan demanded.

Seconds ticked by.

So they were tougher than he'd guessed.

He placed the jewels away, back in their velvet wrappings, and turned to face the couple head-on. "It's obvious you're laundering these jewels through Athena's Creations and the jewels are changing hands even after you procure them."

Mrs. Landrenau darted a look around as if seeing things Dylan didn't, which was quite possible. Who knew how many items had come through Athena's boutique before OFFSUS was brought on site.

"You're giving these items to somebody to sell, and I don't think it's to fund a second honeymoon to Europe. But you can't embezzle from the bank anymore—oh yes, did you think we didn't know about that?" He watched the banker's face grow purple. "So you had to turn to this. What exactly are you funding?"

"Give us those jewels now!" The man motioned to one of his bodyguards, who raised his weapon and trained it on Ben.

Dylan acted, lunging forward and clipping the guard in the back of the thigh with his knife. The guy went down on one side, jamming the knife even farther home. It dug into the muscle, throbbing with his heart as it embedded deep in the femoral artery.

Mrs. Landrenau screamed, and her husband knocked her to the floor as he squeezed off a shot. In a blink, Chaz reared up and got him around the neck. The shot went wild, ricocheting off a steel post and striking glass.

Dylan swore he heard a cry from the office, from the closet. And fury hit. He stomped on the banker's arm, forcing him to drop the weapon as he broke several fingers and probably his wrist too.

"Don't kill him yet, Chaz. Remember what we say." Dylan looked into his brother's furious eyes.

"Let them die slowly," Chaz drawled.

Dylan might have laughed if the situation wasn't the furthest thing from funny ever. All their lives were on the line and the woman he loved was hiding in the closet in the other room.

Ben got one of the bodyguards on the floor and zip-tied his hands and feet together before he could

196

probably even think of his own first name. Sean rushed the other, wrestling for the weapon aimed at his midsection.

Elise popped up from behind the counter, took aim and shot. The man dropped and didn't move again.

"Thanks, *cher*. But when we get home, I'm laying you across my knee and spanking your ass for not heeding my warning to stay behind the counter." Sean rolled to his feet and dumped the clip from the thug's weapon.

Dylan stared down the Landrenaus. "One of your men is dead—or more, judging by the silence in the back room."

The banker's eyes slid to the other side of the showroom where his people should be entering now if Dylan wasn't right.

"The only thing that's going to save your lives now is to work with us. Or do you think the people you're funding will be happy to hear you failed?"

Mrs. Landrenau held up both hands in surrender, several rings glinting on her fingers.

Dylan whipped out his own zip-ties. "The Knight Ops thank you for your cooperation. Captain Ben Knight will be your tour guide. Enjoy your time with the US government interrogators."

Chapter Nine

The closet door opened, but it wasn't Dylan standing there looking down at her.

"Elise." Her name came out shaky on Athena's lips as her newfound friend reached into the closet for Athena's hand.

Elise gripped it and hauled her to her feet. Shaky and swaying, Athena put a hand to her forehead, holding tears at bay. "Where is he? Where's Dylan?"

Her voice held a frantic edge, and she couldn't even touch on the thought that he'd been the recipient of one of those bullets she'd heard zinging around her boutique.

"He had some business to tend to. You can come out now. It's all clear." Elise walked to the door and led the way.

When she stepped out into her showroom and saw even more destruction than the Knight Ops team had wreaked the first time, she stumbled to a halt. Looking around at shattered glass and bullet holes in the side of a counter and a wall by the front door.

And blood.

No bodies littered the floor, but she could see the clear outline of where one had been.

She slapped a hand over her mouth, bile rushing up her throat. "Where is he?" she repeated.

"He's all right." Elise touched her shoulder. "I promise he's all right. He had to debrief—they all did—but they'll be back soon."

"Oh my God. It was really the Landrenaus the whole time?"

"Looks that way. C'mon, sit down. Let me start a pot of coffee."

She took the stool behind the counter and while Elise went off to brew much-needed coffee, Athena looked down to see the velvet open on the surface. The jewels were gone.

Of course, they were evidence. This whole boutique was evidence. How could she ever look at it the same way again? Would she be able to move on with her world and happily dress customers for a living? Her mind was too shocked to think straight about the future of her shop.

Then there was Dylan.

A minute later, Elise returned with a foam cup of steaming coffee. She placed it in Athena's hands and watched as she sipped it.

"Well, the cat's out of the bag now. Or the baby is." She rubbed her belly.

Athena blinked away some of the cobwebs clouding her mind. "What?"

"Sean spilled the news to the guys that I'm expecting. I give it an hour before it reaches Ellietta and Chip."

"Who?" She wrapped her cold fingers around the cup, but it was no substitute for Dylan's warmth.

"Mr. and Mrs. Knight. You'll be meeting them soon, I'm sure. Along with the twins. They're wild, both of them, and did you know Chaz has been dating an old high school crush?"

She shook her head, half aware that Elise was talking nonsense, everyday things with her just to keep her mind off the wreck that was the rest of her life.

"And Roades hasn't exactly settled down yet but give him time. He's such a sweetheart—probably more romantic than any of the others. Whoever finally gets Tyler to settle down has his work cut out for him, but Lexi will be fine. She's savvy and knows what she wants. That's half the battle, right?"

Elise dipped her head to look into Athena's eyes. "You okay, hon?"

She nodded.

"You know what you want, don't you?"

She dropped her gaze to the coffee. The warm brown depths wafted with the nutty tones she loved every morning. But even more than her first coffee of the day, she loved waking next to Dylan.

She wanted that for the rest of her life.

She nodded. "I do know. I want Dylan. I'm in love with him."

Elise's gaze slipped over Athena's shoulder and she smiled. "I'll leave you two alone."

Athena gasped, jumping off the stool and spilling her coffee in the process. But what did a puddle of coffee matter when her floor was covered in glass and blood?

Dylan rounded the counter and took her by the hands. He led her to the front door and kept walking right through it, without locking it, without looking back.

"But...what about my shop?"

"We've got people in there. Next time you see it, it will be back to normal. Right now I need you."

His words slicked through her insides like warm honey, and she focused on the heat of his callused fingers wrapped around hers. To her surprise, he put her in the car and drove her the few blocks to her apartment.

"Why are we here? Is it safe?"

"Anybody associated with this act has been placed under arrest and you're as safe as you were before we barged into your boutique." He opened the apartment door and swept his gaze around, though. She had a feeling he'd do that anyplace she entered, including the bathroom.

He drew her into her own space, and the familiar smells of home brought tears to her eyes. He closed the door and bolted it. Then he took her by the hand.

"*Cher*, what I want from you right now is too much for you to process. So I have to leave."

She shook her head, curls cascading over her shoulders. "What?"

"We were thrown together into this mess, and I can't let you make decisions about your feelings for me until you've had time to process. Distance, space."

He was leaving her?

"No..."

"Fuck, I don't want that either but it's best. Believe me, we both need it." He swallowed hard as if the words were rocks in his throat.

"Dylan, what are you saying?"

He grabbed her by the shoulders and crushed her to him. But only briefly. Too quickly, he stepped back. Eyes burning, he continued to move away from her, leaving her standing alone in the middle of her beloved apartment that didn't seem so fantastic now without him.

She took a step, and he threw up a hand to stay her. She stopped in her tracks.

"You'll be okay, Athena. Elise will check in with you. And... we'll be watching."

Chapter Ten

Athena walked back into her boutique and saw everything put to rights—glass cleaned up, blood vanished and even every single camera hole patched.

She turned in a circle. "My God." How had they done this in a day's time?

They're the freakin' government, that's how. They have every string to pull at their fingertips.

Looking toward her office, her heart gave a heavy thump. For days Dylan had been found sitting there, monitoring her universe. When she walked through the door, she braced herself for what she'd see but it still struck like a blow.

She gripped the doorframe and stared at the neat, cleared desk. Not a technical device in sight.

Oh God. Tears bit at the backs of her eyes but she pushed them down, unwilling to cry. She'd done enough of that the previous night after Dylan had walked out of her life. After the first hour of shock, she'd felt more alone than she ever had in her life. And for a woman without family or many friends, that was a huge deal.

Then her emotions had slowly shifted to anger, and she didn't even have the man nearby to let him have it. Unfortunately, her final drop on this roller coaster was sadness, which was obviously still controlling her.

She turned from the office and walked back out into the showroom. Going through the motions of opening the shop took no brainpower at least. As Mardi Gras week began to close, she would be less busy and hopefully by the end of the day, go home to that soaker tub.

But that brought visions of Dylan at her apartment and his comments about how beautiful her bathroom was. The man's intelligence and knowledge of the world rocked her in a way she'd never known before, and that had nothing to do with the fear and adrenaline of the past week.

She understood his reason for giving her space, but dammit, what if she didn't want it?

The first customer took all the energy Athena had to give, and each one after sapped a bit more life from her. By lunchtime, she felt like a wilted flower. So when Elise breezed in looking elegant and glowing, Athena hurriedly grabbed a set of chignon sticks and wound her hair into a twist on the back of her head.

Elise gave her a small smile, looking too closely at her face and probably making out the hollows under her eyes or the redness from lack of sleep and crying.

"You okay, hon? What am I saying? I can see you aren't."

Athena bit her lower lip. "I'm not quite myself yet."

She nodded. "Understandable. Things like this would shake you up."

"I don't know how you and the Knight Ops live it daily."

She flashed a white smile. "I don't know how you work with these customers all day! That one blonde who wanted you to custom embroider a parade float on her pants in one day?" Elise raised her brows and opened her eyes wide.

Athena laughed, and it felt good but not exactly real either. "It happens. Given another few days, I could have done the job."

"See? That's amazing to me."

They stared at each other. Athena's eyes flooded with tears again. Hopeless, stupid tears. One dribbled down her cheek, and she gave a big sniff. "I don't even know why I'm crying."

"Don't you?" Elise placed a hand on hers.

"It can't be because of Dylan. I hardly know him. He was just... just..." Everything.

Elise's eyes burned with sympathy. "The Knight boys know how to sweep a woman off her feet and alter her life forever. Believe me." She patted her still flat stomach.

Athena shook her head. "What I was feeling can't be real."

"That's why Dylan took some time away, right?"

She sniffled. "It's the right thing to do. I just need a few more days to recover. Last week was like being really sick and shuttled around to doctors and hospitals, enduring fear and worry. Then it's all over and I'm suddenly better, but I'm still feeling the aftereffects of the time."

Elise busted out laughing. "Oh I love it! You're comparing Dylan to a disease."

Athena giggled. "I guess I am."

Elise's expression grew more serious though the twinkle still lit her eyes. "What you need to decide is if you want to live with that disease every day of your life."

She bit into her lip again, an action she'd done so many times today that the flesh was getting sore. "What I'm not sure about is if I can live without it."

"I know the feeling. Sean has scared me so many times I've lost count. When I don't know where he is or if he's okay. I wouldn't know if something happened to him until it was too late." She trailed off, staring across the showroom. After a few seconds, she shook herself and looked directly into Athena's eyes. "That is a real concern you need to consider, Athena. You can even ask Ben's wife Dahlia. Living with a military man has its ups and downs. Question is, can you live with the low points?"

Athena rubbed away the wetness on her cheeks and reached for a tissue. She didn't have any answers to that right now. Changing her entire life to allow a man like Dylan into it wasn't something she could decide right away.

And he was a damn genius for knowing that before even she could realize it.

"I guess I have a lot of thinking to do."

"Thinking goes better over coffee and donuts. Why don't I run down the street to that bakery and see if they have anything left?"

"Knowing your powers of persuasion, you'll have them whipping up a fresh batch of donuts and heating the oil." Athena gave her a watery smile. "Go on—we could use some snacks to go with our girl talk."

Already at the door, Elise tossed a look back at Athena. "I'm here for you."

When she walked out again, Athena smiled through her tears at this new friendship found in the strangest of places. But she couldn't help but think that Elise was a Knight also and if things worked out between her and Dylan—if she chose him and all the baggage he brought along in the package deal—that they'd be sisters-in-law.

She realized she wasn't just in love with Dylan. She was in love with his family too.

* * * * *

Dylan peered through the sights, held his breath and squeezed of the shot. Followed by three more perfect placements on the moving targets at the gun range. A whoop went up behind him from one of his brothers.

When Dylan lowered the rifle, he swung around to look at the group gathered behind him.

"When did you get here?" He checked the chamber and fed it a few more shells.

"Right after you started tearing up the course, bro." Chaz folded his arms and studied him. Dylan ignored it—and the other four sets of eyes trained on him—and resumed his shooting practice.

Pretty soon the guys got in on it too and bets were placed. Ben and Sean were deep in conversation about who was going to kick whose ass. When Ben won by literally a hair's width on the center ring of the target, Sean turned the bet to catfishing.

Roades snorted. "Pretty easy to call that one— Sean's the best."

Sean braced his legs wide and folded his arms, a smug expression on his face. "That's right, boys. Start forking over the cash now."

"Nobody agreed to a fishing tournament," Rocko added, as laid back as always.

"Jackson is entering the one you won last year, Sean. Better not enter this time," Ben warned.

"Colonel Jackson fishes? I thought all he did was barbecue and polish his medals." Chaz's words got a laugh from everybody but Dylan.

He didn't have much to laugh about right now. Feeling as low as the belly of a slug, he was only living moment to moment, trying like hell to keep his mind off Athena. Two weeks had passed and he'd vacillated from resignation that he'd already lost her to determination to win her back. But so far, he'd kept his word by staying away from her. Giving her space and time was essential.

What was that shitty saying about loving something and setting it free, and if it came back to you it was really yours?

He popped off another shot, right between Ben's and Sean's bullet holes.

"Good thing fishin' is only a hobby to Dylan. If he set his hand to it, we'd all be at the bottom of the list," Roades drawled.

Ben took a chair and stared at Dylan until he arched a brow in question. "You got somethin' to say, just say it."

"Fine, I will," Ben said. "How long are you going to go on being a dick? I shoulda let Jackson punish you for that stunt at the fair."

Dylan might have roused to that accusation if he had the energy for anything but dwelling on his own pain. He gazed back. "What am I being a dick about? Haven't I done my job? Hell, I had all of your backs in Mississippi two days ago and the day before that when we raided that dump of a bar."

"Fuckin' Mississippi," three of the guys echoed.

"Your performance is fine, even if there's a lack of heart," Ben said.

209

"Lack of heart? What's heart gotta do with defusing bombs and rounding up assholes with too many guns and not enough brains?"

"We all know what's eating at you, man. Just go get your woman and tell her that you want it all so we can get back on track. One guy's attitude throws us all off." Sean's advice slammed Dylan. But it wasn't anything he hadn't already thought a million times the past two weeks.

"Look," Ben said, "you have to know what Athena will say sometime. Putting it off for longer isn't going to make her decision any different. By now, she's figured out what she wants."

Sean nodded. "Elise says so too."

Dylan jerked his head around to pierce his brother in his gaze. "Elise has been talking to Athena about us?"

"Girl talk."

He didn't know if that made him feel better or worse. Nobody was more on the Knights' side than Elise, but she would share all the cons of loving a man like him. But that wasn't why he'd walked away from her. He needed her to think on things, to know what was in her heart, truly.

"I guess it's good that Elise is telling her all the bad stuff about being in a relationship with me so she can make informed decisions." He pushed out a sigh. He didn't sound convinced and wasn't going to pretend he felt it either.

"Elise thinks she's lonely."

"Athena said that?" His gut churned.

"No, but think about it. She doesn't have siblings or family. She's pretty much devoted to that boutique and lives vicariously through her customers and the events they attend." Sean cleared his throat. "Speaking of clients, the woman who requisitioned the shoes from Athena was finally found." The Landrenaus had given her name and location the same day of their arrest but it had taken the FBI much longer to track her down.

But now that all the players on the chess board had fallen, Athena was completely safe.

Dylan found his breath trickling out and his mind running forward, to driving to her apartment and finally setting eyes on the woman who owned his heart.

He stood and handed his rifle to Chaz. "Your turn. I've gotta run into the city."

He took two steps before Chaz called out, "You wouldn't be visiting a certain clothing boutique, would you?"

Dylan kept walking without looking back. "Yep. Going to find my heart like you guys said."

At times like this, he wished he wasn't so damn practical-minded in driving a compact car. Because right about now, he could use a vehicle with some speed.

In the parking lot, he scanned his brother's rides—Chaz's Jeep, Sean's El Camino and Roades' Ninja.

A grin split his face as he took the keys to his car from his pocket and placed them above the visor. Then he swung his leg over the bike, settled the helmet in place and leaned forward to fiddle with the wiring. The engine started in seconds, and he kicked off at the same moment he hit the gas.

The bike zoomed through the lot and when he got to the highway leading back to New Orleans, he really opened it up. His brother would be pissed but he'd get over it. Someday Roades would have a woman of his own to go crazy over and understand.

By the time he reached the city streets, Dylan had thought of every scenario possible when he walked up to Athena's door. The good, the bad and the ugly were all present in his mind. He only hoped for one outcome, and the little sassy boutique owner had no clue she held his fate so tightly gripped in her hands.

Drawing up next to the curb, he cut the engine and removed his helmet. When he dismounted from the bike, he didn't want to admit his legs felt a bit wobbly from the fear surging through him.

If she turned him away…

He had to be prepared for that. Sean hadn't told him where Athena's thoughts lay, but probably because Elise hadn't been told either.

It was down to him and Athena.

He approached the door.

Athena answered the knock on her door, heart pounding a bit too fast. Each time she heard her backdoor buzzer, she thought of Knight Ops breaking into her boutique and upending her world. And when a pizza was delivered, her palms felt clammy with fear that it could be someone besides the delivery person.

So when she spotted Dylan outside her door, she sucked in a sharp gasp.

A thrill hit her chest, and the quake in her limbs was undeniable. She backed up, rattled, just staring at the man she had wanted nothing more than to set eyes on for weeks.

Her throat closed off on a cry that was never emitted.

His gaze lit on her, touching her like a brand. "Can I come in?"

She stepped back, words jumbled in her mind, and he entered. He seemed to take up so much more space than she remembered. The distance between them had made him shrink and swell in her mind depending on the day, but now that he was standing in front of her, he was larger than life.

Pressing her fingertips to her lips, she tried to breathe.

"I couldn't stay away anymore," he said quietly.

213

She made an involuntary noise in her throat.

"And I hope you don't want me to stay away anymore, Athena."

She simply shook her head.

"*Cher*, the past few weeks have killed me. I know how I feel about you, more than ever. It's stronger than ever." He held her stare. "Are you ready to make a decision about us too?"

"Dylan... God, it's so good to see you!" She threw herself at his chest, and he caught her around the middle, lifting her and swinging her in a half circle as he crushed his mouth over hers. Claiming her completely.

She locked her arms around his neck and kissed him back with everything inside her. "I know you'll go away from me again and again to do your job, but Dylan, don't ever walk away like that. Promise me."

Between biting kisses that were quickly steamrollering them toward the bedroom, he said, "Never. *Mon Dieu,* does this mean you're mine? That you share my feelings?"

"I love you," she cried as he found her throat and nibbled down the column.

Stilling, he lifted his head and met her gaze. Heat rippled through them, an electricity so tangible it felt like she'd touched a bolt of lightning. "I love you too, *cher.*" He let her go and sank to one knee.

Her mind fluttered over what was happening, like a hummingbird's wings beating too fast to see.

214

"Dylan..."

He pulled something from his pocket and opened his palm. In the center were the wedding rings—simple bands that had been tarnished from sitting in the safe the last time she'd seen them.

"Ou se flè mwen ki fleri nan kè mwen." The words fell from his lips as if they were his native tongue. Then he repeated them in English, "You are the flowers that bloom in my heart."

She fought for breath that wasn't thick with tears.

"And I love you. We haven't known each other long, but I don't need more time to figure out how I feel. You're it for me, *cher*. I want to hold on to you for the rest of my life."

"Oh Dylan." She dropped to her knees with him. "I don't think this is just a passing thing, something born from the situation."

"It isn't. I'm not lying when I say you're the flowers that bloom in my heart." He placed the ring on her finger and folded her fingers around it. "I want to marry you. I want to take care of you always and protect you forever."

A rough giggle burst from her, and she clapped a hand over her mouth. His eyes were bright as he studied her. "I hope it doesn't come to more protection. I've had enough for a lifetime." She took the other wedding band from him and slipped it over his pinky finger, the only one it would fit.

215

He flashed a grin—that crooked one that melted her every single time.

She slipped her arms around his neck and he lowered his mouth to hers even as he gained his feet. Lifting her into his arms, he carried her to her bedroom. He already knew the way.

* * * * *

"You didn't say yes to my proposal yet," he said between deep kisses that had his body enflamed with need. "If you need more time—"

"I know the perfect dress."

The air punched from him, followed by a wallop of joy so huge that he felt he was soaring through the sky. "Is that a yes?"

She pushed on his chest, forcing him to roll onto his back. Then she settled atop him, straddling his hips, and started tearing at his belt. "Definitely a yes."

Her silky fingers breached his underwear and he sucked in sharply. "Hell yeah. Take out my cock, bride to be."

Eyes flashing, she wiggled down his body as she drew his shaft from the folds of his clothing. Hot breath washed over the mushroomed tip, and his eyes slipped shut on a prayer for control.

As soon as her sweet lips wrapped around the head of his cock, he bucked upward. Sinking deeper into her mouth at the same time she sucked him right

216

to the root. He felt the tip bump the back of her throat and groaned.

He sank his fingers into her hair and guided her up and down, to work his cock with her hot mouth until his fist was balled and he was shaking.

"Fuck, no more. Come up here."

She moved upward, and he tossed her into the bed, ripping off her clothes. He had to sit up to untie the laces of his combat boots—precious seconds that he wasn't pleasuring her lost.

She giggled.

He paused to stare into her eyes. "What is it?"

"I think we just got the speed record for getting naked."

"*Cher*, we're going to work on that time. Every. Chance. We. Get." He slipped his hand between her legs, and she parted her thighs. Tossing her head back as he reached her soaking pussy.

Need spiked in his core, and he ground his teeth against the need to take, take, take the way his body was demanding him to.

But the passion darkening her eyes made his heart flip again, and he slowed down. Riding one finger up along her seam to the bundle of nerves at the top. She cried out as he drew a circle around it and then depressed it softly into her body.

She dragged her nails over his shoulders. "Dylan!"

"How many times can I do this before you come for me?" He circled again. And again. Her clit swelled under his touch, giving him a power he'd only felt in battle.

Juices slicked his fingers, and he teased her more. Splaying his hand, he stroked her clit with his thumb, sank one finger into her pussy and then hesitated.

They'd never had ass play or even discussed it, but he wanted to give her the trifecta of pleasure, and that could only happen by .

He coated his pinky in her juices and then watching her face, eased it into her ass.

She tensed and cried out, thrashing against his hand.

"Jesus, have you been fucked here before?"

She shook her head wildly, mouth open on an O of ecstasy. "No, but whatever you're doing, I feel like I'm going to shatter. Don't stop, babe. Don't stop!"

Warmth licked through his arm and all through his body. He withdrew both fingers and she mewled. Then he slid them back in. She was so soaking wet, noises of arousal filling the room and her scents like a brain block to him. He could only feel and react.

She lifted her hips off the bed to meet his thrust, and he thumbed her clit over and over. Her inner walls clutched at his fingers, forcing a growl from his throat.

"Hell, you're squeezing me so tight."

"I need to take your cock."

A rough noise erupted from him, more animal than human. "Not until you come apart for me." He doubled his efforts, his hand soaked with her need. When her stomach dipped on a gasp, he knew she was close.

"Dylan. Oh my God." She arched her neck, and he sucked her nipples into his mouth as she started coming. The waves seemed to last forever. She rose and fell on his hand, and he didn't stop until the final shudder left her.

Before the fog cleared from her eyes, he flipped her atop him. "Fuck, I love seeing you right here."

"I don't care about a condom, Dylan. I'm clean."

His mouth fell open. "*Cher*, are you sure?"

She nodded.

"You could be carrying my baby by the time you pass out with pleasured exhaustion."

She ran her hands up her torso to her breasts, cupping them. "I don't mind. Do you?"

His answer was to take her by the shoulders and seat her on his cock. She slid over him, and he found his hands shaking again as he wrapped them around her waist and urged her to move.

* * * * *

Call her reckless, but ever since Elise had talked to Athena about the Knights being so virile, she wondered what would happen if she took that chance with Dylan. And since they were marrying soon anyway, birth control didn't seem to matter.

Besides, now that she'd felt him without barriers, she was never, ever going back.

He moved her up and down on his cock. Each downstroke had her insides squeezing his head as he stretched her. And his fingers working her nipples was something she never wanted to end.

The passion inside her for this man tripled until she lost herself in watching the pleasure cross his rugged features. He bucked upward, and she rocked her hips.

"Dammit, I'm gonna blow. I'm gonna come in you so deep, *cher*."

She flattened her palms on his broad chest and road him faster, pushing him to the same end he'd given her over and over again.

A low groan burst from his lips, and she felt him shudder. The first splash of hot cum soaked her insides, driving her to her own orgasm. She peaked fast and hard.

"God, yes. Fuck me harder," she cried out.

He jerked up into her, his cum mingling with her juices. Five more pulsations and she fell forward, hair hanging around them.

He grabbed her by the nape and yanked her mouth to his. The kiss was wild but soon their releases ebbed, and they slowed. Tangling tongues.

"I fucking love you so damn hard," he grated out.

"I can't believe how fast it all happened."

"I can. I know what I want when I see it."

She nibbled his lower lip, pulling another growl from him. Damn, she loved that sound and vowed to get him to make it every day.

"Since we met, it feels like I've been in a whirlwind."

"It'll only get worse from here, *cher*."

"Which will be worse, meeting your family or telling them we're getting married?"

He flashed that crooked grin that melted her all over again. "Or telling them you're carrying my child."

"You don't know that."

He nodded. "If you aren't right now, you will be by the time the sun comes up."

"I'm not in a rush to start a family, but I don't regret feeling you—all of you." She moved slowly, and his still-hard cock slid through her inner walls.

They shared a moan.

He eased into her and withdrew twice before she leaned into kiss him. With her lips brushing his, she said, "That thing you did with your fingers… do you think you can do it again first?"

"Oh hell yeah." He tossed her off him and into the mattress, following her down. Kissing her until she was gasping and then easing his hand right where she wanted it. Dizzy with desire, she gave herself up to sensation.

Epilogue

"We'd better not be getting any phone calls out here today." Dylan lifted the beer to his lips, his gaze locked on his beautiful fiancée lounging in one of the chairs on the dock several feet away. Lexi said something to her, and she smiled.

Dylan couldn't feel happier than he did right at this moment. He had everything a man could want—a fishin' rod and a beer in hand and an amazing woman at his side.

Ben bobbed his head in agreement at Dylan's words. "I could use a few days of peace and quiet with no interruptions. Just good food, fishin' and hot nights."

Sean chuckled. "TMI, bro. But I'm with you both."

"Hell, I didn't even put a ring on anyone's finger yet, and I'm still satisfied with the fishin' and food." Roades scrubbed a hand over his jaw, thick with beard growth. He'd been letting it go more and more, not that their captain was going to say anything. Ben looked as scruffy as Roades.

Elise came up behind Sean and rested a hand on his shoulder. "Hey, babe, I'm going inside to lie down."

He twisted, squinting into the sun behind her. "Want some company?" Before she answered, he stood and took her by the hand.

"See ya later." Dylan raised the beer to his lips again, a smile spreading over the rim.

Chaz took Sean's place on the edge of the dock, his bare feet dangling near the water. "Could one of you guys give me a hand changing the brakes on my Jeep this week?"

"I'll do it," Rhodes said.

"Thanks. I need it in top shape for a road trip."

All the brothers turned to him. "What road trip?"

"The one I'm taking along the coast."

Dylan eyed him. "I'm assuming there's a woman involved?"

"Could be." He drank off half of his own beer.

Their *maman* got off her lounge chair, patting Athena's shoulder as she passed. She crossed the deck in a swirl of thin cotton skirt and leaned into the center of the group of her boys.

"Who's got an appetite? I'm going inside to heat up that gumbo."

"*Maman*, I'll take anything you put in a bowl and devour it gladly." Dylan grinned up at her, and she patted his cheek. "You need a shave." She looked from face to face. "All of you do."

"Athena likes me a little unshaven," Dylan said.

She sat up with a gasp and lowered her sunglasses to stare at him wide-eyed. He chuckled, and their *maman* just shook her head at their antics.

"I'll pretend I never heard that and know nothing about it." But the way she caught their father's eye made Dylan think otherwise.

Lexi swung her legs over the side of her lounge chair. "When is Rocko coming?"

Ben and Dylan exchanged a look. "Rocko's coming?" Dylan asked.

"I didn't invite him," Ben muttered. "Dammit, I'm going to have to break his legs, aren't I?"

Lexi set her hands on her hips and gave them all a look that would sear the hide off lesser men. But the Knights were made of tougher stuff.

Dylan caught Athena's eyes and she gave a smile that had his pulse thumping faster. The moment swelled until they both stood. The deck was only a few feet, but it was too much for Dylan. By the time he pulled her into his arms, he was aching.

"Let's find a nice quiet place to take the pirogue."

Her gaze shifted to the flat-bottom boat tied to the dock. Her smile widened, and she nodded. "I'll grab a blanket."

He released her and watched her hips twitch as she crossed the deck to the cabin. Having her here with him was the best thing a man like him could ask for. In his line of work, he couldn't promise tomorrow. But with Athena waiting for him, he was

225

determined to make the most of every minute he had on earth with her. Hopefully, someday they'd be sitting here at this very cabin surrounded by grandbabies.

Roades nudged him from his thoughts. "I'll tell *Maman* to save you some gumbo."

He chuckled. "Yeah, do that." Athena emerged just then, her curls bouncing around her beautiful face. Dylan's heart swelled to twice its size—as did another body part.

He took the blanket from her and laid it in the pirogue. Then he took her hand and helped her into it before climbing in behind her. Roades untied the rope and pushed them off.

As they moved through the water, Dylan could see his family getting up to go into the cabin. Athena reached over, her soft fingers stroking over his jaw. She leaned in to brush her lips across his once, twice. Burning need enveloped him, and he yanked her across his lap.

A giggle escaped her, and her eyes danced with happiness and love.

"God, I don't deserve you. After what I did to you, barging into your life..."

She chewed her lower lip and then released it. "It was a terrifying time of my life, and I'm still not entirely recovered. I keep watching every customer who walks into my boutique, waiting for them to try to involve me in some criminal activity. But Dylan, I don't believe things happen randomly. You were brought to me for a reason. We might not have ever met any other way."

"This is why I love you so much."

"That's all?" She arched her back, bringing her breasts in contact with his chest.

He chuckled. "There's that too and so much more."

"Hurry up and find some dry land because I don't think we can rip off each other's clothes in this shaky boat."

He waggled a brow. "We can try."

She batted at his arm. "Get me to dry land so you can take me, Dylan."

He wasn't going to stall another second. He grabbed the pole and dug it into the thick swampy bottom of the bayou and pushed off, propelling the pirogue forward. He knew one small plot of ground with enough shade to keep the blazing Louisiana sun from scorching them. Since the storms had cleared, they'd been left with true Cajun weather.

When he helped her step out of the pirogue, he yanked her right into his arms. Body flush to his, he stared deeply into her eyes. A curl fluttered forward, and he brushed it back with his knuckles.

"I'm not sure if I can wait any longer to marry you."

A joyous smile spread across her full lips. "We want your sister there. And she won't be in boot camp much longer."

He sighed. "I guess it just gives us more practice before the honeymoon."

"Mmm, I like your thinking." Easing her hand around his shoulders, she drew him down until their lips connected. Warmth gripped him, and he took control of the kiss, showing her just how hungry he was to get started on their plan.

READ A SNEAK PEEK OF AFTER MIDKNIGHT

Roades had just completely and catastrophically ended his career. One fucking misstep had almost blown up the whole mission in the faces of the elite Knight Ops team. If not for his teammates, all would have been lost, and thank God they'd pulled it out of their asses at the last minute.

But Roades' head was still on the chopping block, and Colonel Jackson had a cleaver in his hand.

Okay, it was just a file but if it was Roades', then it was thick from other times he went off the rails and took matters into his own hands. He wasn't some young pup anymore, and he knew how to follow orders. What had gotten him in trouble was following his gut too, and that might mean the end of his career in the special forces.

The thump of Colonel Jackson's boots as he paced the room in front of Roades was a constant drum in his chest. He held the salute for one minute... two. His arm was beginning to ache, and Jackson knew it. Still, the colonel wasn't going to give that *at ease* anytime soon. Not when he was fuming and the man to take it out on was Roades.

His biceps started to burn but he'd experienced worse. He held the pose and counted each step the colonel took. He was up to two hundred twelve when Jackson jerked around to face him.

The colonel's stare was direct and piercing. If Roades was a lesser man or even a couple years younger, he might piss his pants. But he was a Knight—and Knights didn't tuck tail and run.

Jackson waved the file in Roades' face, the breeze off it smelling papery and cooling the sweat on his brow. "At ease, you little piss-ant."

Roades dropped into a less formal pose, his muscles thanking him. He dragged in a deep breath and waited for the ass-chewing he was about to receive and then some.

"You realize what you've jeopardized for our division, Knight?"

Yeah, he'd gone in with guns blazing, his sights set on the target... that apparently wasn't the target at all but one of their own undercovers. An agent who'd been working the enemy for nearly a year, easing into a position of trust and regard.

But looking down the barrel of Roades' weapon had made the undercover talk.

Loudly.

"Sir, all due respect but—"

Jackson whirled on him. "You know, every time I hear all due respect from one of you Knight boys' mouths, my teeth just about break off from grinding them. If you respected anything, you would not be in this position right this minute."

"Understood, Colonel, but—"

Colonel Jackson took off pacing again. "But bullshit. You got the wrong mark and therefore the undercover was made."

"There was nothing to tell me an undercover was even on site, sir."

"You knew how sensitive this mission was and you fucked it up."

"I did not fuck it up, sir. We pulled through. The captures were made, the victims recovered and safe." Roades was grinding his own teeth now. Goddamn, he hated being told off, and being youngest of the five brothers, he had a lot of experience at it. Didn't mean he stomached it for long, and he'd been well-trained to be mouthy.

When Jackson stared him down, his eyes were bloodshot, and a vein throbbed in his temple. "Damn, son, you just don't get it, do you? That undercover is now a target of that group, and he cannot go back into service without taking extreme measures. He's lost a year of work finding the man responsible for this crime, was closer to the target than anyone ever has been since the inception of the terrorist group. And you walk in there and pull a gun on him."

"Sir, it isn't my fault he squawked like a parrot, sir."

Jackson stepped up, face in Roades' face. "Are you blaming him, Knight?"

He steeled his spine. "An agent should be prepared to take a bullet if necessary, sir. He wasn't. He collapsed under the pressure, and that is not my fault, sir."

"Jeezus, Knight," Jackson drawled in his Southern Louisiana twang that didn't always come through in orders. "You *are* dumping the blame on the agent. When it was *you* who acted irresponsibly by pulling your weapon in the first place! Were you ordered to pull your weapon?"

Roades didn't even wince in the face of his superior's shouting, nor did he answer the question the colonel already knew. His chest burned with the need to yell back, but this wasn't his commander and big brother Ben. His brother might kick his ass but Jackson could — and most likely would — end his career in the special ops force.

"Sir, I saw my opportunity and I took it. Back in 2011, if that SEAL hadn't seen Bin Laden and taken the chance, we'd still be — "

Jackson jabbed a finger at Roades' face, an inch from his nose. "Not another word, Knight!"

His chest rose and fell with the effort not to spew it back at the colonel. He kept telling himself it was in his best interest to be still and await the punishment he was sure to receive.

Jackson flipped open the file and read a bit on whatever page was on top. His brow creased and he slammed the file shut again. "This is full of your misdemeanors, Knight." He started reciting some, and Roades tuned them all out. Each he'd gotten flack from or even a slap on the wrist, but he wouldn't be so lucky this time.

"What the hell am I going to do with you?" Jackson seemed to speak to himself rather than Roades, so he remained silent.

He could almost hear his brothers chiding him with a *silent for once*. But Roades pushed his brothers from his mind and gazed at the colonel.

"Three months." He held up three fingers, the last three, his thumb and forefinger creating a ring. "Three months off. Your team will receive a replacement until you're off probation."

"Three—"

"Do you want to make it six?"

He gulped down the words he was about to say and stood straight and silent.

Jackson resumed his pacing. "See yourself out, Knight."

He saluted, throat clamped shut on all the crap he'd like to say in retaliation. But he walked out of the building and straight to his bike. The Ninja had earned him his nickname on the team—a name he wouldn't hear for three months.

"Dammit to hell," he muttered and swung his leg over the seat. His team would all still be debriefing, and he didn't know what the hell to do with himself. Three months of being left out of missions, unable to stand up next to his brothers and their teammate Rocko and protect his country.

He ran his fingers through his hair. He'd really fucked up.

Sure, he'd see everyone, but they would be unable to include him in anything classified. And just what the hell was he supposed to do for three months?

He kicked the bike into gear and sped out of the parking lot, ripping between two cars and causing one to lay on his horn. The bike leaned, but Roades was as good as a stunt driver and he whipped it upright to take a turn at high speed.

Reckless, his family would call him, and what the hell did he care right now? He didn't.

He gassed it, and the lightweight bike pulled a wheelie. He rode it out for several city blocks before setting it down. Open road—that's what he needed right now.

With his fists clamped on the grips and his throat burning with a bellow of frustration and fury, he gunned the bike, making his escape from reality for however long he could.

Em Petrova

Em Petrova was raised by hippies in the wilds of Pennsylvania but told her parents at the age of four she wanted to be a gypsy when she grew up. She has a soft spot for babies, puppies and 90s Grunge music and believes in Bigfoot and aliens. She started writing at the age of twelve and prides herself on making her characters larger than life and her sex scenes hotter than hot.

She burst into the world of publishing in 2010 after having five beautiful bambinos and figuring they were old enough to get their own snacks while she pounds away at the keys. In her not-so-spare time, she is fur-mommy to a Labradoodle named Daisy Hasselhoff and works as editor with USA Today and New York Times bestselling authors.

Find Em Petrova at empetrova.com

Other Indie Titles by Em Petrova

West Protection
HIGH-STAKES COWBOY
RESCUED BY THE COWBOY
GUARDED BY THE COWBOY
COWBOY CONSPIRACY THEORY

COWBOY IN THE CORSSHAIRS
PROTECTED BY THE COWBOY

Xtreme Ops
HITTING XTREMES
TO THE XTREME
XTREME BEHAVIOR
XTREME AFFAIRS
XTREME MEASURES
XTREME PRESSURE
XTREME LIMITS
Xtreme Ops Alaska Search and Rescue
NORTH OF LOVE

Crossroads
BAD IN BOOTS
CONFIDENT IN CHAPS
COCKY IN A COWBOY HAT
SAVAGE IN A STETSON
SHOW-OFF IN SPURS

Dark Falcons MC
DIXON
TANK
PATRIOT

DIESEL
BLADE

The Guard
HIS TO SHELTER
HIS TO DEFEND
HIS TO PROTECT

Moon Ranch
TOUGH AND TAMED
SCREWED AND SATISFIED
CHISELED AND CLAIMED

Ranger Ops
AT CLOSE RANGE
WITHIN RANGE
POINT BLANK RANGE
RANGE OF MOTION
TARGET IN RANGE
OUT OF RANGE

Knight Ops Series
ALL KNIGHTER
HEAT OF THE KNIGHT
HOT LOUISIANA KNIGHT
AFTER MIDKNIGHT

KNIGHT SHIFT

ANGEL OF THE KNIGHT

O CHRISTMAS KNIGHT

Wild West Series

SOMETHING ABOUT A LAWMAN

SOMETHING ABOUT A SHERIFF

SOMETHING ABOUT A BOUNTY HUNTER

SOMETHING ABOUT A MOUNTAIN MAN

Operation Cowboy Series

KICKIN' UP DUST

SPURS AND SURRENDER

The Boot Knockers Ranch Series

PUSHIN' BUTTONS

BODY LANGUAGE

REINING MEN

ROPIN' HEARTS

ROPE BURN

COWBOY NOT INCLUDED

COWBOY BY CANDLELIGHT

THE BOOT KNOCKER'S BABY

ROPIN' A ROMEO

WINNING WYOMING

COWBOY SECRET Beck's story
COWBOY RUSH Kade's Story
COWBOY MISTLETOE a Christmas novella
COWBOY FLIRTATION Ford's story
COWBOY TEMPTATION Easton's story
COWBOY SURPRISE Justus's story
COWGIRL DREAMER Gracie's story
COWGIRL MIRACLE Jessamine's story
COWGIRL HEART Kezziah's story

Single Titles and Boxes
THE BOOT KNOCKERS RANCH BOX SET
THE DALTON BOYS BOX SET
SINFUL HEARTS
JINGLE BOOTS
A COWBOY FOR CHRISTMAS
FULL RIDE

Club Ties Series
LOVE TIES
HEART TIES
MARKED AS HIS
SOUL TIES
ACE'S WILD

Firehouse 5 Series

ONE FIERY NIGHT
CONTROLLED BURN
SMOLDERING HEARTS

Hardworking Heroes Novellas
STRANDED AND STRADDLED
DALLAS NIGHTS
SLICK RIDER
SPURRED ON

EM PETROVA
WWW.EMPETROVA.COM

Printed in the USA
CPSIA information can be obtained
at www.ICGtesting.com
LVHW022325020724
784552LV00030B/805